D0379663

THE WRONG BOX

THE WRONG BOX

ROBERT LOUIS STEVENSON & LLOYD OSBOURNE
ADAPTED BY JOSEPHINE OHAYON

SBS SCHOLASTIC BOOK SERVICES
New York • London • Richmond Hill, Ontario

Copyright © 1966 by Scholastic Magazines, Inc. All rights reserved. Published by Scholastic Book Services, a division of Scholastic Magazines, Inc.

1st printing .... ◦⁊◦ ◦⁊◦ ◦⁊◦ ◦⁊◦ ◦⁊◦ ◦⁊◦ ◦⁊◦ .... December 1966

Printed in the U.S.A.

CONTENTS

ong ago, when Joseph and Masterson Finsbury
e little lads, their father, a well-to-do London
chant, had the two brothers join a small tontine.
l he known that this would lead to attacks in the
t and a dubious trafficking in corpses, he might
e reconsidered.

n appearance, a tontine is nothing more than a
p of investors. As the years pass fellow tontiners
off, and the money increases in the common pool.
lly, the grand sum is fluttered in the face of the
weary survivor. By this time he is so old that he
obably deaf and cannot hear of his success. He
so probably dying, or half-dead, so his victory
s something to be desired. The inanity is ob-
: no one concerned profits.

the year 1840 the thirty-seven members of the
ne were all alive. By 1850 their number had de-
ed by six. In the year 1856 to 1857 business
even more lively, for various and bloody wars
ed off no less than nine. By 1870 there remained
ive of the original members. The years slipped
s they have a way of doing, and at the date of
story only three tontiners, including the two
ury brothers, Joseph and Masterson, were still

en Lieut. General Sir Glascow Bigger, K.C.S.I.,
M.G., etc., etc., passed away, there wasn't a per-
all of London who really knew him, or would

CAST OF CHARACTERS

Masterson Finsbury	One of two surviving beneficiaries of a sizeable tontine.
Joseph Finsbury . .	Masterson's brother; the other beneficiary left in the tontine; a bumbling bore.
Morris Finsbury . .	A nephew and ward of Joseph's.
John Finsbury . . .	Morris' brother; also a ward of Joseph's.
Michael Finsbury . .	Masterson's son; a successful lawyer, known to be "the man for a lost cause."
Mr. Wickham . . .	One of Michael's clients; a young man of wealth and vacant mind.
Julia	Morris' and John's young and pretty housekeeper.
Gideon Forsyth . .	An acquaintance of Michael's; a barrister without a brief; a friend of Julia's.
Edward Hugh Bloomfield . . .	Gideon's rich and generous uncle who aids both Julia and Gideon.
William Dent Pitman	Drawing master and friend of Michael's.
John Dickson . . .	Alias of Michael Finsbury.
Ezra Thomas . . .	Alias of William Dent Pitman.

7

CHAPTER I
A Grim Beginni

SHOULD THIS SORDID TALE of th
prove the means of preventing
inexperienced gentleman from
edly into crime, it will not have

For there are times when ev
entertain thoughts of murder,
ted against brother, and tric
streak the land. One of these ti
involved.

tor
cre
wa
car
but
by,
our
Fins
aliv

W
K.C
son

have cared to know him. Indeed, his death was remarked by the only two persons who could profit:
Joseph and Masterson Finsbury. The prize of the
tontine now lay between them.

By this time Masterson was seventy-three years old
and had long since retired from business. He lived
in absolute and utter seclusion with his son, Michael.

Joseph, on the other hand, was still up and about
and presented a familiar, if unpopular, figure on
the streets of London. This was to be deplored because Masterson had led a model British life, and here
he was, age-weary, at seventy-three. Joseph, barely
two years younger, and in the most excellent pres-
ervation, had disgraced himself throughout his life
by idleness and eccentricity.

Originally embarked in the leather trade, Joseph
had soon wearied. A taste for useless information,
not promptly checked, had soon begun to sap his
manhood. There is no passion more debilitating than
that for useless information, except perhaps the itch
for speechmaking. Regretfully, the first passion
usually accompanies the second, and the two had
found a happy marriage in the person of Joseph.

Over the years this double malady had reached its
acute stage. Joseph would travel thirty miles by foot
to deliver a lecture to a kindergarten. These lectures were not meant, he would declare, for college
professors; they were addressed directly to "the

great heart of the people." The heart of the people must certainly be sounder than its head, for Joseph's lectures were received with enthusiasm. His lecture entitled, "How to Live on One Million Pounds a Year," created a sensation among the unemployed; "Education and Its Desirability," gained him the respect of the ignorant.

While Joseph was building up a lively reputation for himself among the more cultivated portion of the illiterate, his domestic life was suddenly overwhelmed by orphans. The death of an obscure brother saddled him with the charge of his two nephews, Morris and John.

Joseph had a kindly disposition and he hastened to make the boys welcome. This was not so much because of blood ties. The leather business—in which he promptly invested his nephews' fortune of £30,-000—had, of late, exhibited unmistakable symptoms of decline. A capable Scot was chosen as manager of the enterprise, and the cares of business never again afflicted Joseph Finsbury. Leaving Morris and John in the hands of the capable Scot, he began his extensive travels on the Continent and in Asia Minor.

He spent many years wandering over the face of the world and returned to England only when Morris and John required his attention. His two nephews had been placed in a good, but economical, school where they had received a sound commercial education. This was somewhat awkward, as the leather business—in which the boys' money was invested—was by no means in a state that invited inquiry.

In fact, when Joseph went over his accounts, preparatory to surrendering the trust, he was dismayed to discover that his nephews' fortune had not increased by his stewardship. Even by transferring every penny he had in the world to Morris and John, there would still be a deficit of £7,800. When these depressing facts were communicated to his two nephews in the presence of a lawyer, Morris Finsbury threatened his uncle with all the terrors of the law. He was prevented from taking extreme steps by the advice of the professional man.

"You cannot get blood from a stone," observed the lawyer.

Morris saw the point and came to terms with his uncle. On the one hand, Joseph gave up all that he possessed and assigned to his nephew any profits from the tontine. This was already quite a hopeful speculation, as Joseph was certain to outlive his brother Masterson. On the other hand, Morris agreed to provide for his uncle.

In a large, dreary house on John Street, Bloomsbury, the three dwelt together; a family in appearance, in reality a financial association. Joseph was, of course, a slave. John, a gentleman with a taste for the music hall, the Gaiety bar, and the sporting papers, was a man of absolutely no distinction.

The cares and delights of empire passed directly to Morris. He was a bitter man. Summoning the servants in the morning, he doled out the needs of the day with his own hand. He watched the consumption of the sherry and numbered the biscuits. Painful scenes took place over the weekly bills, and the cook was frequently impeached. The shopkeepers came and bickered with Morris over a question of three farthings. A superficial person might have called him a miser; in his own eyes he was simply a man who had been defrauded. The world owed him £7,800, and he intended that the world should pay.

But it was in his dealings with Joseph that Morris' character particularly shone. Joseph *must* outlive his brother Masterson and collect the prize of the tontine. Everything depended upon it.

Old Joseph was seen monthly by a doctor, whether he was well or ill. His diet, his clothing, his outings, were carefully supervised. In bad weather he was kept in the house. In good weather, by half-past nine, he must be ready in the hall. Morris would see that he remembered his gloves and scarf. Then, the pair would start out for the leather business, arm in arm.

It was a dreary trip since no love was lost between the two. Morris would never let his uncle forget that he had defrauded him. Joseph, though he was a mild enough soul, regarded his nephew with something very near to hatred. But the trip there was nothing in comparison to the trip back. The mere sight of the leather business, now on the brink of financial ruin, was enough to poison the life of any Finsbury.

Joseph's name was still over the door; he still signed the checks. This was only policy on the part of Morris, who wanted to give the impression that Joseph would live to the ripest possible age. In reality, the business belonged entirely to Morris and in it he found an inheritance of sorrows. He tried to sell it, but the offers he received were quite scornful. He tried to expand it, but it was only the liabilities that he succeeded in expanding. He tried to restrict it, but it was only the profits that he managed to restrict.

Nobody had ever made money out of the leather business except the capable Scot, who retired—after his discharge—and built a castle with his profits. Morris would revile the memory of this man daily, as he sat in the private office opening his mail, with old Joseph at another table, sullenly awaiting orders or savagely affixing his signature to he knew not what.

Business hours in the Finsbury leather trade had been cut to the barest minimum. Even Morris' strong sense of duty to himself could not force him to dally within those walls and under the depressing shadow of that bankruptcy. Presently, Morris would lead his living investment back to John Street. Then, having entombed Joseph in the hall, he would depart for the day in quest of seal rings, the only passion of his life.

Had Joseph steeped his hands in gore, he would still not deserve to be thus dragged at the heels of young Morris. He was made to sit captive in the halls of his own leather business, was subjected to mortifying comments on his whole career. Every five minutes his clothing was carefully examined, his collar pulled up, the presence of his mittens verified. He was taken out and brought home in custody, like an infant with a nurse. At the mere thought of it, his soul would swell with venom. He would hasten to discard the abominable coat and the detested mittens. Then he would slink upstairs to the privacy of his own bedroom. Here, at least, Morris would not venture. Joseph would settle down among his notebooks, register disconnected facts and calculate insignificant statistics.

Here too he would sometimes lament his connection with the tontine. If it were not for that, Joseph thought, Morris would not care to keep me. I might be a free man. I could so easily support myself by giving lectures. The amount of information that I have in my power to convey is a thing that beggars description.

Then one day Morris had an idea. Why not, he thought, try to reach a compromise with Masterson and his son Michael. They could all split the prize of the tontine. Since Joseph and Masterson were the only surviving members, certainly they could reach an agreement that would benefit them all. Morris, suddenly beholding his £7,800 restored to him, hastened to Michael's office. The sun shone, birds were singing, and the future looked bright for Morris Finsbury.

Michael was something of a public character. Launched upon a law career at a very early age, it was not beyond him to engage in shady affairs. He was known to be the man for a lost cause. He could extract testimony from a stone and interest from a gold mine. Consequently, his office was besieged by that class of persons who still have some reputation to lose, and find themselves in risk of losing it. In private life Michael was a man of pleasure, but even pleasure can have sobering effects. What is more to the point, he had never seemed to take the Finsbury tontine too seriously.

So it was with little fear that Morris presented himself in Michael's office and proceeded feverishly to describe his scheme. For hours Michael allowed him to dwell upon the limitless advantages of such a compromise. Then, Michael rose from his seat, uttering a single clause.

"It won't do, Morris."

In vain Morris pleaded and reasoned and returned day after day to plead and reason. In vain he offered a bonus of £1,000, of £2,000, of £3,000. In vain he offered—in Joseph's name—to be content with only one third of the tontine. Still there came the same answer: "It won't do."

"I don't understand," he said at last. "You answer none of my arguments; you haven't a word to say. I believe it's malice."

"You may believe one thing," replied Michael, "whatever else I do, I am not going to gratify any of your curiosity. You see, my dear cousin, this is our last interview upon the subject."

"Our last interview!" screeched Morris.

"I can't have my business hours encroached upon. I am a busy lawyer. Incidentally, have you no business of your own? Is there no profit to be made in the leather trade?"

"I believe it to be malice," repeated Morris doggedly. "You have always hated and despised me."

"No, no—not hatred," said Michael soothingly. "I rather like you. There's such an air of surprise about you, you look so dark and attractive from a distance. Do you know that to the naked eye you look romantic, like what they call a man with a past? Indeed, from all that I hear, the leather trade is full of past."

"It's no use talking to you," said Morris, disregarding these remarks. "I shall see your father."

"Oh, no, you won't," said Michael. "No one can see my father."

"I would like to know why," cried Morris.

"I never make any secret of that," replied Michael. "He is too ill."

"If Masterson is as ill as you say," cried Morris, "more the reason for accepting my compromise. I *will* see him."

"Will you?" said Michael, showing Morris the door. Morris left in a rage, vowing that Michael would live to regret his words.

A few days later, on the recommendation of his doctor, Joseph—the poor Golden Goose—was to leave for a vacation at Bournemouth. So, in pursuit of purer air, the family shook off the dust of London. Joseph didn't care where he was as long as pen and ink were available, and he could avoid martyrdom in the office of the leather trade. Morris was content to have a quiet time for thought. His brother, John, a man of city tastes, was in despair.

Morris was prepared for any sacrifice. All he wanted was to get his money back again and to rid himself of the leather trade. It would be strange, indeed, if he could find no way of influencing Michael. "If I could only guess his reason," Morris repeated to himself.

By day, as he walked in the country woods, and by night, as he tossed in his bed, and at mealtimes, when he forgot to eat, that problem was constantly before him: why had Michael refused to compromise?

At last, one night, he burst into his brother's room and woke him.

"What's the matter now?" asked John.

"We return to London at once!" shouted Morris.

"Oh, bravo!" cried John. "But why?"

"I know why Michael won't compromise," said Morris. "It's because he can't. Uncle Masterson's dead, and Michael's keeping it a secret."

"Golly!" cried the impressionable John. "But why does he do it?"

"To cheat us of the tontine," said his brother.

"He couldn't. You have to have a doctor's certificate when a body dies," objected John.

"You've never heard of a crooked doctor?" inquired Morris. "If any man could arrange it, Michael could. He has his plan all worked out. Depend upon it, it's a good one, for he's a clever man. But, I'm clever too. Besides, I'm desperate. I've been defrauded of £7,800."

"Oh, don't be tedious," interrupted John. "You've lost far more already trying to get it back."

CHAPTER II

The Best-Laid Plans

A FEW DAYS LATER, the three males of this highly depressing family were observed boarding the train at Bournemouth. The weather was raw and changeable, and poor Joseph was dressed accordingly. He was outfitted with health boots, his suit was of genuine ventilating cloth, and his shirt of hygienic flannel. He was draped to the knees in his inevitable overcoat of marten's fur. Even the railway porters

at Bournemouth marked the unfortunate Joseph as
a patient of Sir Faraday, the celebrated London
doctor. There was but one evidence of personal
taste: a Siberian hunting cap of moth-eaten fur.
The sentimental value of this hunting cap was con-
siderable, and nothing could divorce Joseph from it.

As soon as the three Finsburys located their compartment, they began quarreling. This little domestic quarrel proved to be Morris' undoing. Had he
lingered a moment longer by the window, this tale
need never have been written. He might have then
observed the arrival of a second passenger in the
uniform of Sir Faraday. The astonished porters remarked upon the appearance of two overcoats of
marten's fur on the same day, but Morris had other
matters on his mind which he judged to be more important.

"I never heard of such a thing," Morris shrieked,
resuming a discussion which had scarcely ceased all
morning. "The check is not yours, it's mine."

"It is payable to me," replied Joseph, with an air of
bitter obstinacy. "I will do what I please with my
own property."

The check was for £800. It had been given to
him at breakfast to endorse, and he had simply
pocketed it.

"Hear him, Johnny!" cried Morris. "His property!
The very clothes on his back belong to me."

"Let him alone," said John. "I am sick of both of you."

"That is no way to speak of your uncle," cried Joseph. "I will not endure this disrespect. You are a pair of exceedingly forward, impudent, and ignorant young men, and I have quite made up my mind to put an end to the whole business."

Morris looked uneasily at his uncle. This unusual act of insubordination in regard to the check had already troubled him, and now these mutinous words sounded ominously in his ears.

Upon one occasion many years before, when Joseph was delivering one of his insufferable lectures, the audience had revolted. Finding Joseph somewhat dry, they had taken the question of amusement into their own hands. Joseph was driven from the scene. Morris had not been present on that fatal day, but if he had, he would have recognized a certain fighting glitter in his uncle's eye and a certain chewing movement of his lips. But even to people not acquainted with Joseph, these symptoms breathed of something dangerous.

"Well, well," said Morris. "I have no wish to bother you further till we arrive in London."

Joseph did not so much as look at his nephew. With trembling hands, he pulled his overcoat of marten's fur tight around him, produced a copy of the *British Mechanic,* and began leafing savagely through its pages.

"I wonder what's making him so cantankerous?" wondered Morris. "I don't like the look of it at all."

The train traveled forth into the world, bearing along its cargo of anonymous passengers, among these old Joseph, engrossed in his paper, and John, slumbering over the articles in *Naughty London by Night,* and Morris, his peace of mind troubled by a dozen grudges, suspicions, and alarms. It passed Christ Church by the sea, Herne with its pinewoods, Ringwood on it winding river. A little behind time, it drew up at the platform of Browndean station.

Many passengers put their heads out of the windows, and among them the old gentleman dressed like Joseph in the uniform of Sir Faraday. Protected against the bitter wind by his overcoat of marten's fur, he too was returning from a vacation at Bournemouth. Alone in life, this seedy traveler could vanish from the face of the earth, and none would be the wiser. Perhaps the old gentleman thought something of the sort, for he looked melancholy enough as he pulled his bare, gray head back into the compartment, and the train rolled on, with ever-quickening speed, across the mingled heaths and woods of England.

Not long after Browndean, the train screeched

unexpectedly to a brutal halt. A sudden jarring of brakes set everybody's teeth on edge. Morris Finsbury was aware of a confused uproar of voices and sprang to the window. Women were screaming, and men were tumbling from the windows onto the track as the guard cried to them to stay where they were. At the same time the train began to gather speed and move slowly back to Browndean. But at the very next instant, all these various sounds were blotted out by the screeching whistle and the thundering onslaught of the down express.

Morris did not hear the actual collision. Perhaps he fainted. He had a wild dream of having seen the train double up and fall to pieces. Sure enough, when he regained consciousness, he was lying on the bare earth and under the open sky. His head ached savagely. He wiped his hand across his forehead and was not surprised to see it red with blood. The air was filled with an intolerable, throbbing roar, which he expected would die away with the return of consciousness. Instead, it seemed to swell louder and to pierce more cruelly through his ears. It was a raging, bellowing thunder, like a boiler-riveting factory.

As curiosity began to stir within him, he sat up and looked about. The track ran in a sharp curve around a wooded hill. All of the near side was heaped with the wreckage of the Bournemouth train.

The wreckage of the express was mostly hidden by the trees. Just at the curve, under clouds of vomiting steam, lay what remained of the two engines. Everywhere, people were running back and forth, crying aloud, and many others were lying motionless like sleeping tramps.

Morris suddenly drew an inference. "There has been an accident!" he thought and was elated at his insight.

A moment later he sighted John, who lay close by as white as a sheet. "Poor old John!" he thought and he took his brother's hand in his with childish tenderness. It was perhaps the touch that brought John to his senses. He opened his eyes, sat suddenly up, and after several moments of stunned silence, finally managed to ask, "What's all the excitement about?"

The unearthly roar still thundered in their ears. "Let's get away from that," Morris cried, pointing to the vomiting steam that still spouted from the shattered engines. The two brothers helped each other up, and stood quaking and wavering at the scene of death all around them.

Just then they were approached by a group of men already organized into a rescue party.

"Are you hurt?" cried one man, a young fellow with sweat streaming down his face. From the way he was treated, he was evidently the doctor.

Morris shook his head, and the young man nodded grimly.

"We need every man we can get," he said. "There's terrible work before us, and nobody should shirk."

The doctor was hardly gone before Morris awoke to the full possession of his wits.

"Uncle Joseph!" Morris cried. "Where is he?"

"Uncle Joseph!" parroted John. "Where can he be? He can't be far away. I hope the old boy isn't damaged."

"Come and help me look for him," ordered Morris, with an air of savage determination strangely foreign to his character. "If he's dead!" he cried and shook his fist at heaven.

The brothers hurried back and forth, staring in the faces of the wounded, or turning the dead upon their backs. They examined hundreds of people and still there was no trace of Uncle Joseph. Their search brought them near the center of the collision, where the boilers were still blowing off steam with a deafening roar. It was a part of the field not yet reached by the rescue party. The ground was very rough. It was a place where many bodies might lie concealed, and they hunted frantically for any clue. Suddenly Morris paused, pointing his index finger with a tragic air. John followed the direction of his brother's hand.

At the bottom of a sandy hole lay something that had once been human. The face had suffered severely, and it was unrecognizable. But the snowy hair and the overcoat of marten's fur identified the body as Uncle Joseph's. The Siberian hunting cap must have been lost in the crash, for the dead man was bareheaded.

"The poor old man!" cried John, with feeling.

But there was no sentiment at all upon Morris' face as he gazed upon the dead. Gnawing his nails, with eyes turned inward, his forehead marked with the stamp of tragic indignation, he stood there silent. He had been defrauded of his inheritance while he was an orphan at school, he had become involved in that decadent leather trade, and his cousin Michael was trying to cheat him out of the tontine. He had borne all this with dignity. But here was the final injustice: they had gone and killed his uncle!

"Here!" he ordered suddenly. "Take his heels. We must get him into the woods. I'm not going to have anybody find him."

"What's the use?" asked John.

"Do what I tell you," cried Morris, as he took the corpse by the shoulders. "Do I have to carry him myself?"

They were close to the edge of the woods. In a few minutes they were undercover. A little farther back, in a sandy clearing, they laid their burden down, and stood and looked at it with loathing.

"What are you going to do?" whispered John.

"Bury him, of course!" replied Morris. He opened his pocketknife and began to dig feverishly.

"You'll never get anywhere with that," objected his brother.

"If you won't help me, you blundering coward," screamed Morris, "you can go to the devil!"

"It's all madness," said John, "but no man shall call me a coward," and he began to help Morris grudgingly.

The soil was sandy and light, but matted with the roots of the surrounding firs. As they baled the sand from the grave, it was often discolored with their blood. An hour passed of boundless energy on the part of Morris, of lukewarm help on the part of John. Still the trench was barely nine inches in depth. Into this shallow grave the body was flung. Sand was piled upon it, branches from the nearby firs were added, and still from one end of the sordid mound a pair of feet projected and caught the light upon their patent-leather toes. But by this time, the nerves of both brothers were badly shaken. Even Morris had had enough of the grisly task, and they both skulked off like animals.

"It's the best that we can do," said Morris, sitting down.

"And now," began John, "perhaps you'll have the politeness to tell me what it's all about."

"Upon my word," cried Morris, "if you do not understand by now, you never will!"

"Oh, of course, it's some rot about the tontine," replied John. "But what's the use? We've lost it, and that's the end of that."

"I tell you," said Morris, "Uncle Masterson is dead. Michael is keeping it a secret. He's tricky and he wants the prize of the tontine at any price!"

"Well, now Uncle Joseph is dead too," said John.

"He's not dead unless I choose to make the fact known," replied Morris.

"If that's so," cried John, "if you're right, and Uncle Masterson has been dead all along, all we have to do is tell the truth and expose Michael."

"You seem to think Michael is a fool," sneered Morris. "Can't you understand that he's been preparing this fraud for years? He has the whole thing ready: the crooked doctor, the undertaker, the phony certificate all ready except for the date! Let him get wind of this business, and you mark my words, Uncle Masterson will die in two days and be buried in a week. But you listen to me, Johnny. What Michael can do, I can do. If he plays a game of bluff, so can I. If his father is to live forever, by God, so shall Uncle Joseph. The tontine is not lost yet!"

"It's illegal, isn't it?" ventured John. "And then suppose you're wrong? Suppose Uncle Masterson's alive and kicking?"

"Well, even then," replied Morris, "we are no worse off than we were before. In fact, my plan improves our position. Uncle Masterson must die some day. As long as Uncle Joseph was alive, he might have died any day. But there's no problem now, no limit to the game of bluff I propose. As far as Michael ever has to know, Uncle Joseph will live forever!"

"I don't know if it will work," sighed John. "You were always such a bungler, Morris."

"I'd like to know what I ever bungled," cried Morris.

"Well, you know, there's the leather trade," suggested his brother. "That's considered somewhat of a financial disaster."

It was a mark of self-control in Morris that he let this insult pass unchallenged.

"Now, about the business at hand," began Morris. "Once we can get the corpse home to Bloomsbury, there'll be no more problem. We'll bury him in the cellar. It's perfect for it. Then all I have to do is find a crooked doctor."

"Why can't we leave him where he is?" asked John.

"Because we know nothing about this part of the country," retorted Morris. "This neck of the woods may be a regular lovers' lane. I don't want some romantic pair stubbing their toes on Uncle Joseph's corpse. Now, start thinking about the real problem. How are we going to get the body home?"

Various schemes were aired. The station at Browndean was, of course, out of the question. It would, most likely, now be a center of curiosity and gossip. John feebly proposed buying a huge cask and sending it as beer, but the objections to this plan were overwhelming. The purchase of a packing case would arouse suspicion, since why should two gentlemen without baggage of any kind need a packing case?

"We must tackle this problem more logically," cried Morris at last. "Suppose now," he added excitedly, speaking in fits and starts as if he were thinking aloud, "suppose we rent a tiny cottage in some deserted spot. It's a small price to pay when you consider the tontine. There's nothing unusual about new tenants buying a packing case. Tomorrow, we'll bring the packing case over to the nearest railroad station and ship it to London. At last, Johnny, I believe I've hit the nail on the head."

"Well, it does sound more feasible," admitted John.

Everything agreed upon, they returned to Browndean in search of a hearty meal and a suitable cottage. It's not always easy to find a secluded cottage at a moment's notice, but, for once, fortune smiled on Morris and John Finsbury in the form of a deaf carpenter. This carpenter was a man rich in cottages of the required description and he was all too eager to satisfy their request.

The second cottage they visited, placed, as it was, about a mile and a half from any neighbors, caused them to exchange a glance of hope. On closer inspection, the cottage was not without depressing features. It stood in a marshy-looking hollow of a heath. Tall trees shut out the light and surrounded the place with an eternal aura of gloom. The roof was obviously rotting away. The walls were stained with unwholesome splashes of green. A strange chill and haunting damp smell pervaded the kitchen. Poor Morris viewed the tiny rooms, the low ceilings, and the sparse furniture with something akin to dismay. The bedroom boasted of only one bed.

With the intention of getting the place more cheaply, Morris remarked on this one defect.

"Well," retorted the man, "if you both can't sleep in the same bed, you'd better consider one of my fancier residences. They're a bit more expensive, of course."

"What's more," pursued Morris, "there's no water. How do you get your water?"

"We fill *that* from the spring," replied the carpenter, pointing to a big barrel that stood beside the door. "The spring ain't so *very* far off, everything considered, and it's easy to carry the water in buckets. There's a bucket over there."

Morris nudged his brother, but John was already putting two and two together. The barrel was practically new. If the two brothers had had any reservations about the cottage, they were quickly dispelled at the sight of the solidly-built barrel. A price was agreed upon, the keys were presented with great ceremony, and scarcely an hour later the Finsbury brothers felt quite at home. Nor was that all that they had accomplished. They had already hired a sturdy two-wheeled cart. Yes, thought Morris optimistically, things were certainly looking brighter.

John began to prepare afternoon tea. Meanwhile, Morris, rummaging about the house, was delighted to discover the barrel's lid on the kitchen shelf. The barrel was complete. Blankets would take the place of straw. As the difficulties began to vanish from his path, Morris rose almost to the brink of exultation. There was, however, one difficulty not yet faced, one upon which his whole scheme depended. Would John agree to remain alone in the cottage? He had not yet dared to ask the question.

Tea was poured with a festive air.

"Indeed," cried John, "I always said that a barrel was what you wanted for this business."

"Of course," said Morris, thinking this a favorable opportunity to prepare his brother, "of course you must remain here until I send for you. I'll tell everyone that you and Uncle Joseph are still vacationing in the country. We couldn't both appear in London at the same time. They would all wonder what happened to the old man. In a business of this kind, it's never a wise policy to arouse suspicion."

John's jaw dropped.

"Oh, come on!" he cried. "You can stay in this hole yourself. I certainly won't."

Morris flushed with anger. He saw that he must win John at any cost.

"You must remember, Johnny," he said, "the amount of the tontine. If I succeed, our bank accounts will profit."

"But if you fail," retorted John, "what about our bank accounts then?"

"I'll pay all expenses," said Morris, after an inner struggle. "You'll lose nothing."

"Well," said John, with a laugh, "if the expenses are yours, and half the profits are mine, I don't mind remaining here for a couple of days."

"A couple of days!" roared Morris, who was beginning to get angry and controlled himself with difficulty. "This is monstrous. I take all the risks. I pay all the expenses. I divide the profits. You won't make the slightest effort to help me. It's not decent. It's not honest. It's not even kind."

"But suppose," objected John, who was considerably impressed by his brother's vehemence, "suppose that Uncle Masterson is alive after all, and lives ten years longer. Must I rot here all that time? No tontine is worth it!"

"Of course not," replied Morris soothingly. "I only ask a month. By that time, I will have found out if Uncle Masterson is really dead. If he is still alive, after a month's time you can travel abroad."

"Travel abroad?" repeated John eagerly. "Why shouldn't I go now? Tell 'em that Uncle Joseph and I are living it up in Paris."

"Nonsense," said Morris.

"Look around," pleaded John. "It's this house, it's such a pigsty, it's so dreary and damp. You said yourself that it was damp."

"I only said that to the carpenter to reduce the rent," replied Morris. "Now that we're all settled, I've seen worse."

"And how will I amuse myself?" complained the victim. "How can I entertain a friend?"

"My dear Johnny, if you don't think the tontine is worth even a little inconvenience, say so, and I'll give this deadly business up."

"You're certain about the amount of money in the tontine, I suppose?" asked John. "Well, send me a copy of *Naughty London by Night* and all the comics regularly. I'll face the music."

As the afternoon wore on, a creeping chill arose from the marsh and invaded the cottage. The fire smoked, and a shower of rain tingled on the windowpanes. At intervals, when the gloom deepened toward despair, Morris would produce the whiskey bottle. More time passed, a candle flickered, and the approach of dusk added a touch of tragedy.

"I can't stay here a month," cried John suddenly. "No one could. The whole thing's nonsense, Morris."

In reply, Morris soothingly proposed a bit of supper and another drink. All was in readiness. The barrel, as if it knew what fate had in store, rested uneasily on the cart. Before long, the two brothers set forth on their adventure under a starless heaven.

CHAPTER III
Uncle Joseph Escapes

IT IS NOT SURPRISING that Joseph Finsbury had often entertained ideas of escape. His lot was not a happy one. Morris was hardly the model nephew. As for John, if he was the only link that bound one to home, most people would vote for foreign travel.

Joseph's plan, or at least the temptation, was already months old, and when a check for £800, payable to himself, was suddenly placed in his hand, it simply brought matters to a head. He pocketed the check and awaited the right moment. As things turned out, he didn't have long to wait.

He was one of the first persons to recover after the train crash. He scrambled to his feet, noticed his prostrate nephews, and fled. For a man of seventy, the victim of a railroad accident, and encumbered with an overcoat of marten's fur, fleeing is not easy. Luckily, the woods were close by. Joseph hobbled toward the safety of the woods with extraordinary speed. Being somewhat winded and a good deal shaken, he stretched out in the first clearing he reached and fell promptly asleep.

Life is a morbid business: while Morris and John were digging in the sand to conceal the body of a total stranger, Uncle Joseph lay in dreamless sleep only a few hundred feet deeper in the woods.

He was awakened by sounds from the highway. Joseph stood up, shook the dirt from his overcoat, and walked in the direction of the noise. Soon he was on the highway, looking to the east and west from under his Siberian hunting cap, pondering what to do next.

A sound of wheels rose in the distance, and then a cart was seen approaching. It was well filled with parcels and driven by a good-natured-looking man. On its side was painted: I. CHANDLER, DELIVERIES.

Mr. Chandler was perhaps a little puzzled to find so old a gentleman, so strangely clothed, begging for a ride on such a remote road. But he was a kindly man, glad to be of service, and he offered Joseph a seat. He had his own idea of civility, and he asked no questions. Silence, in fact, was quite good enough for Mr. Chandler. But the cart had scarcely begun to move forward when he found himself involved in a one-sided conversation.

"I can see," began Joseph Finsbury, "by the parcels and boxes that are contained in your cart, each marked with its individual label, and by the horse you drive, that you occupy a post in that great English system of transport, which, with all its defects, is the pride of our country."

"Yes, sir," agreed Mr. Chandler vaguely, not knowing quite what to reply.

"I am an open-minded man," continued Joseph. "In my youth, I traveled far and wide. Nothing was too small or too obscure for me to acquire. At sea I studied seamanship, learned the complicated knots employed by mariners, and acquired the technical terms. At Naples, I learned the art of making macaroni. At Nice, I studied the principles of making candied fruit. I never went to the opera without first buying the libretto."

"You must have seen a great deal, sir," remarked Mr. Chandler, prodding his horse along. "I wish I could have had your advantages."

"Do you know how often the word 'whip' occurs

in the Old Testament?" inquired Joseph. "If I remember exactly, one hundred and forty-seven times."

"Do it indeed, sir?" said Mr. Chandler. "I never would have thought it."

"The Bible contains three million five hundred and one thousand two hundred and forty-nine letters. Of verses, I believe that there are upward of eighteen thousand. There have been many editions of the Bible. However, the 'Paragraph Bible,' as it is called, is a well-known edition, and it is so called because it is divided into paragraphs."

Mr. Chandler stifled a yawn, replied that he thought that was only logical, and turned his attention to the more immediate task of passing a cart of hay. It was a matter of some difficulty, for the road was narrow, and there was a ditch on either side.

"I see," began Joseph, when they had successfully passed the cart, "that you hold your reins with one hand. You should use two."

"Well, I like that!" replied the downtrodden Mr. Chandler. "Why?"

"You do not understand," continued Joseph, barely stopping for breath. "What I tell you is a scientific fact, based on the theory of the lever, a branch of mechanics. There are some very interesting books on the subject, but I fear that you are not very well read. We have now driven together for some time, and I cannot remember that you have contributed a single fact. To return to the point, I do not know if you observed that you passed the hay cart on the left side?"

"Of course I did," cried Mr. Chandler, who was now getting belligerent. "He'd have the law on me if I hadn't."

"In France, now," resumed Joseph, "and also, I believe, in the United States of America, you would have passed on the right."

"I would not," replied Mr. Chandler, shifting restlessly on the bench. "I would have passed on the left."

"I observe," continued Joseph, not bothering to reply, "that you mend the dilapidated parts of your harness with string. I have always protested against the carelessness of the English poor. In their private and domestic life, as well as in their work, the lower classes of this country are improvident, thriftless, and extravagant. A stitch in time . . ."

"Who the devil *are* the lower classes?" cried Mr. Chandler. "You are the lower classes yourself! If I thought that you were a blooming aristocrat, I would not have given you a ride."

The words were spoken with undisguised ill-feeling. It was obvious that the two men were not compatible and further conversation was out of the question.

With an angry gesture, Joseph pulled his cap over his eyes. Then, producing a notebook and a pencil from one of his pockets, he soon became absorbed in calculations.

Mr. Chandler glanced at his companion with mingled feelings of triumph and alarm. Triumph because he had succeeded in checking that endless flow of speech, and alarm lest, by any accident, it should begin again. The remainder of the trip was endured by both in silence, and it was still in silence that they drove into Southampton.

Dusk had fallen. The shop windows glimmered in the streets of the old seaport. In the houses, lights were kindled for the evening meal. Joseph Finsbury began to think complacently of his night's lodging. He put his notebook away, cleared his throat, and looked doubtfully at Mr. Chandler.

"Will you be civil enough," he said, "to recommend an inn?"

Mr. Chandler pondered for a moment.

"Well," he said at last, "the Tregonwell Arms might do."

"The Tregonwell Arms will do very well," replied Joseph, "if it's clean and cheap, and the people are civil."

"I wasn't thinking so much of you," said Mr. Chandler thoughtfully. "I was thinking of my friend, the innkeeper. He's a special friend of mine, you see, and I'd like to keep him for a friend. I was thinking, would it be fair to saddle him with an old fellow like you, who might be the death of him with useless information. Would it be fair to the inn?" inquired Mr. Chandler, with an air of candid appeal.

"Now listen here," cried Joseph. "It was kind of you to bring me here for nothing, but it gives you no right to talk to me like that. Here's a shilling for your trouble. If you do not choose to drive me to the Tregonwell Arms, I can find it myself."

Mr. Chandler was surprised and a little startled by the outburst. Muttering something apologetic, he returned the shilling. They drove in silence through the twisting lanes and narrow streets. Finally, they drew up before the bright windows of an inn.

"Is that you, Chandler?" cried a hearty voice from the stable yard. "Come in and warm yourself."

"I only stopped here," Mr. Chandler explained, "to deposit this old gent. He'd like food and lodging. Mind, I warn you against him. He'll talk your ear off."

The friendly innkeeper, in spite of Mr. Chandler's less than complimentary introduction, treated Joseph with the utmost courtesy. He led him into the back room, where there was a big fire burning in the grate and a table was spread.

An hour later, Joseph rose from supper a giant refreshed. He changed his seat for one nearer the fire. The beginnings of a speech had already begun to fester in his fertile brain. He had a captive audience, all workingmen. But even workingmen have to be courted, and there was no man more determined than Joseph Finsbury. He placed his glasses on his nose, drew a bundle of papers from his pocket and spread them before him on a table. He crumpled them, he smoothed them out. First he skimmed over them, apparently well pleased with their contents. Then, tapping his pencil and contracting his brows, he seemed to reconsider some particular statement.

A stealthy glance around the room assured him of the success of his maneuvers. All eyes were on the performer. Mouths were open, pipes hung suspended. The birds were charmed.

"I observe," said Joseph, addressing the innkeeper, but taking the whole room into his confidence at the same time with an encouraging look, "I observe that some of these gentlemen are looking with curiosity in my direction. Yes, certainly it is unusual to see anyone immersed in literary and scientific labors in the middle of a public inn. But I have some calculations here that I made this morning upon the cost of living in this and other countries. This is a subject, I need scarcely to say, of great interest to the working classes. I will begin, gentlemen, with the income of eighty pounds a year."

With less compassion than he would have had for

brute beasts, Joseph delivered all of his tedious calculations. He occasionally gave nine versions of a single income, placing the imaginary person in London, Paris, Bagdad, Spitsbergen, Bassorah, Heligoland, the Scilly Islands, Brighton, Cincinnati, and Novgorod. His audience was fascinated, then stunned. Not one of them had ever spent such a deadly evening.

Long before Joseph Finsbury had reached Novgorod, the company had dwindled to a few diehards and the bored innkeeper. There was a constant stream of customers from the outer world, but after five minutes of the tiresome Joseph, they departed with the utmost speed for the next inn.

By the time the imaginary man was vegetating in the Scilly Islands, the innkeeper was left alone with the speechmaker. The imaginary person had scarcely begun his life in Brighton, when even the hardy innkeeper couldn't stand it any more; he went to bed.

Joseph Finsbury slept soundly that night. He awoke late, and, after a good breakfast, ordered the bill. But it is one thing to order the bill, and quite another to pay it. The total was small, but Joseph's available assets were smaller. He called the innkeeper.

"Here is a check for £800," said Joseph. "I am afraid, unless you can cash it, that I may be detained here."

The innkeeper looked at the check.

"You might be detained here?" he said, fearfully repeating Joseph's words. "You have no other money with you?"

"Some trifling change," replied Joseph. "Nothing to speak of."

"Then you can send it to me. I shall be pleased to trust you."

"To tell the truth," said Joseph. "I am rather inclined to remain here for a while. I am in need of funds."

"If a loan of ten shillings would help you, I am at your service," cried the innkeeper, eagerly.

"No, I prefer to stay," said Joseph, "and get my check cashed."

"You shall not stay a minute more in my inn," screeched the innkeeper. "This is the last time you shall have a bed at the Tregonwell Arms."

"I insist upon remaining," cried Joseph. "Throw me out if you dare!"

"Then pay your bill," said the innkeeper.

"Take that," cried Joseph, tossing him the check.

"It is not legal tender," replied the innkeeper. "You must leave this inn at once."

"You cannot appreciate the contempt I feel for you," said Joseph. "I refuse to pay my bill."

"I don't care about your bill," said the innkeeper. "All I want is your absence!"

"That you shall have," cried Joseph. "Would you at least inform me of the time of the next train for London?"

"It leaves in exactly three quarters of an hour," replied the innkeeper. "You can easily catch it."

Joseph's position was not an enviable one. On one hand, it would have been advisable to avoid the railway. Morris and John were most certainly lying in wait for his recapture. On the other hand, it was necessary to get the check cashed before Morris stopped payment. He decided to leave on the first train. There remained but one point to be considered: how to pay his fare.

For once, Joseph's overcoat of marten's fur proved an asset. The stationmaster, recognizing Joseph as a man of no little means, smilingly assumed all responsibility.

As Joseph sat awaiting the moment of departure, he witnessed an incident strangely connected with the fortunes of the Finsburys. An enormous packing case, addressed to WILLIAM DENT PITMAN, ARTIST was being hoisted into the baggage car by a dozen tottering porters. In the very next corner of the car was jammed a barrel bearing the label MORRIS FINSBURY, 16 JOHN STREET, BLOOMSBURY, LONDON. HANDLE WITH CARE.

The egg of a grisly tale lay unhatched.

CHAPTER IV
The Man
with Roving Fingers

WITH NO TIME TO SPARE, Michael Finsbury, the lawyer, and his client, Mr. Wickham, caught the London express. A spasm of running had brought them on the platform just as the engine uttered its departing snort. There was only one compartment easily within their reach. They had sprung into it, but Michael had no sooner had his feet upon the ground when he sighted the sleeping Joseph.

"Great Guns!" he cried. "Uncle Joseph! This will never do!"

He backed out, almost upsetting his companion, and once more closed the door upon his relative.

The next moment, the pair jumped into the baggage car.

"Why all the excitement?" inquired Mr. Wickham. "Does your Uncle Joseph object to smoking?"

"He's a man to be avoided," replied Michael.

"Cantankerous old fellow, eh?" suggested his companion.

"Not in the least," said Michael. "It's simply that he has a solid talent for being a bore. Can't control the powers of his tongue. Rather cheery, I dare say, on a desert island, but on a train journey, unbearable. You should hear him on the subject of tontines. Joseph's a fanatic. He and my father are neck and neck on the homestretch: the prize of the tontine lies between them."

"By Jove!" cried Wickham. "Then your father is Masterson Finsbury of the Finsbury tontine! I never would have guessed it!"

"Ah!" replied Michael. "Do you know that old boy, my dear uncle, is worth £100,000 to me? There he was asleep, and no witness but you. But I spared him, because murder is a dirty business."

Mr. Wickham, pleased to be in a baggage car, was flitting back and forth like a gentlemanly butterfly.

"By Jove!" he exclaimed. "Here's something for you! 'Morris Finsbury, 16 John Street, Bloomsbury, London.' Is this Morris a relative of yours?"

"My cousin and Uncle Joseph's keeper," replied Michael. "He has a bossy disposition, but he's a little afraid of me."

"What a lark it would be to change the baggage labels," chuckled Mr. Wickham. "By George, we could send these things skipping all over England. It'd take years to straighten the mess out!"

At that moment, the conductor, surprised by the sound of voices, opened the door to the baggage car.

"You had better step in here, gentlemen," he said, after hearing their story.

"Won't you come along, Wickham?" asked Michael.

"I'll stay on in the baggage car," replied Mr. Wickham.

And so for the rest of the journey, Mr. Wickham remained with the baggage. Smitten with the desire to shine in Michael's eyes and prove himself a person of humor, Mr. Wickham was no sooner alone when he began prancing from box to box changing labels.

As the train pulled into the London station, he rejoined Michael. His face was flushed from the exertion, and his cigar was almost bitten in two.

"By George, this has been a lark!" he cried. "I've sent the wrong thing to everybody in England. This cousin of yours, Morris of Bloomsbury, has a barrel big enough to house a corpse. Some lucky party will be surprised to find that on his doorstep!"

It was useless to try to be serious with Mr. Wickham.

"Be careful," said Michael. "I am getting tired of your perpetual scrapes. My reputation is beginning to suffer."

"Your reputation will be all gone before you finish with me," replied his companion with a grin. "Add it to my bill. 'For total loss of reputation, six and eightpence.'"

"It strikes me," said Michael, lighting a cigar, "that you must be a cursed nuisance in this world of ours."

"Do you really think so?" exclaimed Mr. Wickham, delighted with the compliment. "Yes, I suppose that I am a nuisance. But, mind you, even the smallest breeze can give rise to a hurricane."

CHAPTER V

The Plot Thickens

GIDEON FORSYTH WAS A HAPPY ENOUGH young man. He would have been happier if he had had more money and less uncle. One hundred and twenty pounds a year was the total income from his law practice, but his uncle Hugh supplemented these meager earnings with a handsome allowance and a great deal of advice. This advice was usually framed in language that would have been judged unseemly on board a pirate ship. Poor Gideon's career had failed miserably. Worse yet, Uncle Hugh had implied that either things improve or Gideon must prepare to live on his own money.

No wonder Gideon was moody. He had not the slightest desire to change his present habits. But that was no argument, since the withdrawal of an allowance by his uncle would revolutionize them still more radically. His lifelong friend, Michael Finsbury, had tried to help him find clients, but where Michael met with success, Gideon met with failure. How to get a client? That was the question.

There was but one bright candle in Gideon's dark world. Her name was Julia. Life had not been kind to the penniless Julia. For longer than she cared to remember, she had worked as a housekeeper for Morris Finsbury. It had been a nightmare.

About three o'clock on the eventful day when Mr. Wickham had changed the labels in the baggage car, Gideon was turning the corner of John Street. Suddenly, he found his path barred by a crowd. A huge moving van was backed against the curb. Half resting on the street, half supported by the glistening moving men, was the largest packing case that Bloomsbury had ever seen. On the steps of the Finsbury residence, the burly driver was arguing with a young girl.

"It is not for us," the girl was saying. "I beg you to take it away. It couldn't get into the house, even if you managed to get it out of the van."

"I'll leave it on the sidewalk, then," replied the driver.

"You must allow me to help you, Miss Julia," said Gideon, putting out his hand.

Julia gave a little cry of pleasure.

"Oh, Gideon," she exclaimed, "I am so glad to see you. We must get this horrid thing, which can only have come here by mistake, into the house. The man says we'll have to take off the door and knock out two of our windows, or be fined for leaving our parcels on the pavement."

By this time, the men had successfully removed the box from the van, had plumped it down on the pavement, and now stood leaning against it, gazing at the door of No. 16 with obvious distress. The windows of the whole street had filled, as if by magic, with curious spectators.

With as scientific an expression as he could assume, Gideon measured the doorway. He then measured the box, and, after comparing his findings, concluded that there was just enough space for it to enter. Next, throwing off his coat, he assisted the moving men in taking the door from its hinges.

At last, the packing case, having mounted the steps

on the backs of the staggering movers, was deposited at the far end of the hallway, which it almost blocked. The men smiled at each other as the dust settled. It was true that they had left the entrance in total ruin and ploughed deep ruts in the wall, but at least they were no longer the public spectacle of London.

"Well, sir," said the driver, "I never seen such a job. Let's go, men."

Gideon closed the door after the fast-departing movers and turned to Julia. Their eyes met and they made the whole house ring with their laughter. Then Julia went and examined the box curiously.

"This is the strangest thing that ever happened," she said with another burst of laughter. "It is certainly Morris' handwriting on the label, but I received a letter from him this morning telling me to expect a *barrel*. Is there a barrel coming too, do you think, Gideon?"

" 'Statuary. Fragile,' " read Gideon aloud from the painted warning on the packing case. "Then Morris told you nothing about this?"

"No. As I said, I expected a barrel," replied Julia. "Oh, Gideon, don't you think we could take a peep inside the box?"

"Yes, indeed," cried Gideon. "Just let me have a hammer."

He worked hard and earnestly. Julia stood silently by, watching the workman rather than the work. After a while, Gideon glanced up from his labors and smiled at her. He forgot to turn away his eyes and, swinging the hammer with energy, discharged a smashing blow on his own knuckles. With admirable self-control, he swallowed an oath and substituted the harmless comment, "Butterfingers!" But the pain was sharp, and his nerve was shaken.

In a moment Julia was at his side with a basin of water and a sponge and had begun to bathe his wounded hand.

"I'm dreadfully sorry," said Gideon meekly. "If I had any manners, I'd have opened the box first and smashed my hand afterward. It feels much better," he added. "I assure you it does."

"I think you are well enough now to direct operations," Julia said. "Tell me what to do, and I'll be your workman."

The bulk of the work had been accomplished, and soon Julia burst through the last barrier. They were knee-deep in straw. A moment later, they were rewarded with a glimpse of something white and polished. An unmistakable marble leg made its appearance.

"He is surely a very athletic person," said Julia.

"I never saw anything like it," added Gideon.

Soon another leg appeared, and then a knotted club resting upon a pedestal.

"It's a Hercules," cried Gideon, "and I'd say that this is about the biggest and worst example of statuary in Europe. Who in heaven's name could have sent it here?"

"I suppose that he was an unwanted gift," said Julia. "And for that matter, I think that we could have done very well without the monster ourselves."

"Oh, don't say that," replied Gideon. "This has been a most unusual afternoon."

"And I don't think that you'll forget it very soon," said Julia. "Your hand will remind you."

"Well, I suppose that I must be going," said Gideon reluctantly.

"No," pleaded Julia. "Why should you? Stay and have tea with me."

"If I thought that you really wished me to stay," said Gideon in a rush, "of course I should be only too willing."

"Why, of course I do," cried Julia. "Let's have it here in the hall amidst the statuary."

"Ever so much the better," exclaimed Gideon.

"Now," said Julia, as she spread the table for tea, "I am going to show you Morris' letter. Read it aloud, please. Perhaps there's something I have missed."

Gideon took the letter and, spreading it out on his knee, read the contents aloud:

Dear Julia,

I'm writing you from Browndean, where we are spending a few days. Poor Uncle Joseph was very much shaken in that dreadful train accident. I'm sure you've read about it in the papers. Tomorrow I'm leaving him with John and returning to London. Before I arrive you will have received a barrel. DO NOT OPEN IT ON ANY ACCOUNT. Just leave it in the hallway.

Morris Finsbury

P.S. Be sure and leave the barrel in the hallway.

"There seems to be nothing in the letter about a statue of Hercules in a packing case," said Gideon. "Would you mind, Miss Julia, if I asked you a few questions?"

"Certainly not," replied Julia, "and if you can explain why Morris sent this packing case with a statue inside instead of a barrel, I shall be eternally grateful."

Gideon was on the verge of replying, when they were both startled by a knocking at the door.

"Oh, Gideon!"

"Don't be afraid, my dear Miss Julia," cried Gideon.

"I know it's the police," she whispered. "They are coming to complain about the statue."

The knock was repeated. It was louder than before, and more impatient.

"It's Morris," cried Julia in a startled voice, and she ran to the door and opened it.

It was indeed Morris that stood before them. Not the ordinary Morris, but a wild-looking man, pale and haggard, with bloodshot eyes.

"The barrel," he cried. "Where's the barrel that came this afternoon?" He stared up and down the hallway, his eyes, as they fell upon the legs of Hercules, literally goggling in his head. "What is that?" he screamed. "What is that statue? Speak, you fool! What is that? Where's the barrel?"

"No barrel came, Morris," replied Julia coldly. "This is the only thing that has arrived."

"This!" shrieked the miserable Morris. "I don't know anything about it!"

"It came with a label in your handwriting," replied Julia. "We had to nearly pull the house down to get it through the front door. That is all I can tell you."

Morris gazed at her in utter bewilderment. He wiped his hand across his forehead and leaned against the wall like a man about to faint. Then, his strength restored, he overwhelmed the trembling Julia with torrents of abuse.

"You shall not speak to Miss Julia in that manner," said Gideon sternly.

"I shall speak to my housekeeper as I like," shrieked the furious Morris.

"Not a word more, sir, not one word," cried Gideon. "Miss Julia cannot stay a moment longer in the same house with you. Come, Miss Julia."

"Gideon," replied Julia, "you are right. I cannot stay here any longer."

Pale and resolute, Gideon offered her his arm. Julia had scarcely handed her key to Morris before an empty carriage drove into John Street. It was hailed by both men, and as the cabman reined in his horse, Morris made a dash for the vehicle.

"Sixpence above your fare," he cried recklessly. "Waterloo Station for your life. Sixpence for yourself!"

"Make it a shilling, Guv'nor," said the man, with a grin, "the young people were first."

"A shilling then," cried Morris, mentally cursing the man.

The driver whipped his horse and the carriage vanished from John Street.

CHAPTER VI
Things Get Worse

AS THE CARRIAGE SPED through the streets of London, Morris tried not to panic. Obviously, his plan had misfired. Somewhere in England was the barrel with the dead body. It was essential to recover it. That much was painfully clear. If, by some stroke of good luck, it was still at the station, all might be well. If it were already in the hands of the wrong person, matters looked more ominous. People who receive unexplained packages are usually keen to open them, and if someone had already opened the barrel . . .

"Main line, or loop?" asked the driver.

"Main line," replied Morris, mentally deciding that the man should have his shilling after all. It would be madness to attract attention.

He passed through the ticket office and wandered disconsolately along the platform. A breathing space in the day's activity had left the station practically deserted. No one seemed to notice him, which was a good thing. On the other hand, he was making no progress in his quest. Something must be done, something must be risked. Every passing moment only added to his dangers. Summoning all his courage, he stopped a porter, and asked him if he remembered receiving a barrel by the morning train.

"I was not here this morning, sir," replied the porter, somewhat reluctantly, "but I'll ask Bill. Do you recollect, Bill, having gotten a barrel from Bournemouth this morning?"

"Oh, the party that received the barrel you mean raised a slight bit of trouble," retorted Bill.

"What kind of trouble?" cried Morris, pressing a penny into the man's hand.

"You see, sir, the barrel arrived at one-thirty. No one claimed it till about three, when a small, sickly-looking gentleman came up, and sez he, 'Have you got anything for Pitman,' or 'Will'm Dent Pitman,' if I recollect right. 'I don't exactly know,' sez I, 'but I rather fancy that barrel there bears that name.' The little man went up to the barrel and seemed all took aback when he saw the address, and then he started thundering at us for not having brought what he wanted. 'I couldn't care less what you want,' sez I to him, 'but if you are Will'm Dent Pitman, there's your barrel.' "

"Well, and did he take it?" cried the breathless Morris.

"Well, sir," replied Bill, "it seems it was a packing case he was after. The packing case came, that's for certain, because it was about the biggest packing case ever I clapped eyes on. This Pitman, he was a good deal wrought up and he found the stationmaster, and they got hold of the head moving man—the one who delivered the packing case. Well, sir," continued Bill, warming to his story, "I never seen a man in such a state. Some gen'leman had slipped him a few shillings, and he had made straight for the public inn. That was where the trouble come in, you see."

"But what did he say?" gasped Morris.

"I don't know that he *said* much, sir," continued Bill. "He had lost his book and all the receipts. He couldn't tell *where* he took the packing case."

"And what did this Pitman man do?" asked Morris.

"Oh, he went off with the barrel, very trembling

like," replied Bill. "I don't believe he's a gentleman in good health."

"Well, so the barrel's gone," said Morris, half to himself.

"You may depend on that, sir," replied the porter. "But you had better see the stationmaster."

"Never mind, it's of no importance," said Morris, and he walked hastily out of the station.

A light rain had begun to fall. London appeared bleak and uninhabited. Looking around in disgust, Morris proceeded to reconsider his position. Suppose he accepted defeat and declared his uncle's death at once? He would lose the tontine, and with that the last hope of his £7,800. Calmly at first, and then with growing enthusiasm, he reviewed the advantages of backing out. It involved a loss, but, come to think of it, not such a great loss after all: only the tontine. The tontine had always been a speculative venture, anyway. He reminded himself of that eagerly. He had never really expected that the tontine business would work out. He had never even very definitely hoped to recover his £7,800. He had been hurried into the whole thing by his cousin Michael's obvious dishonesty. Yes, it would probably be better to stop running after the tontine, settle back on the leather trade . . .

"Great Guns!" cried Morris. "I have not only

not gained the tontine, I have lost the leather trade as well!"

The monstrous fact was all too apparent. He had no power to sign checks. Until he could produce legal evidence of Uncle Joseph's death, he was a penniless outcast. On the other hand, as soon as he produced it, he had lost the tontine! There was no hesitation on the part of Morris. He decided to drop the tontine like a hot potato and concentrate all his efforts on the leather trade and what remained of his small inheritance.

A moment later, he suddenly realized the full extent of his calamity. Declare his uncle's death? He couldn't! Since the barrel with the body was now lost, he had no proof of his uncle's death. Uncle Joseph had, in a legal sense, become immortal.

Morris' head began to spin. Then a remark of his uncle's flashed into his memory: if you want to think clearly, put it all down on paper. "Well, the old boy knew a thing or two," said Morris aloud. "I'll try it, but I don't believe that a paper was ever made that could clear my mind."

He entered the corner inn, ordered bread and cheese, and writing materials, and sat down before them heavily. He tried the pen. It was an excellent pen, but what was he to write? "I have it," cried Morris. "Double columns is the best method!" He prepared his paper and began to write.

Bad	Good
1. I have lost my uncle's body.	1. But then Pitman has found it.

"Wait a minute," said Morris. "I am letting the spirit of contradiction run away with me. Let's begin again."

Bad	Good
1. I have lost my uncle's body.	1. But then I no longer need to bury it.
2. I have lost the tontine.	2. But then I still may save it if Pitman disposes of the body, and I can find a crooked doctor.
3. I have lost the leather trade.	3. But not if Pitman gives the body to the police.

"Oh, but in that case I go to jail. I had forgotten that," thought Morris. "Is there any positive answer to No. 3? Is there any possible good side to such a beastly affair? There must be, of course, or what would be the use of this double-entry business? By George, I have it!" he exclaimed. "It's exactly the same as No. 2!" And he hastily rewrote the passage.

Bad	*Good*
3. I have lost the leather trade.	3. But not if I can find a crooked doctor.

"This crooked doctor seems to be quite a necessary factor," he mused. "First, I want him to give me a certificate that my uncle is dead, so that I may get the leather trade. Then, I want a certificate stating that he's alive—but here we go again with incompatible interests!" And he returned to his tabulation.

Bad	*Good*
4. I have almost no money.	4. But there is plenty in the bank.
5. Yes, but I can't get at the money in the bank.	5. But—that s e e m s unhappily to be the case.
6. I have left the check for £800 in Uncle Joseph's pocket.	6. But if Pitman is a dishonest man, the presence of this check may lead him to keep the whole affair secret and throw the body into the Thames.
7. Yes, if Pitman is dishonest and he finds the check, he will then know who Joseph is and he may blackmail me.	7. Yes, but if I am right about Uncle Masterson, I can blackmail Michael.

8. But I can't black-mail Michael until I find out for sure about Uncle Masterson.

8. Worse luck!

9. The leather trade will soon need money for current expenses, and I have none to give.

9. But the leather trade is a sinking ship.

10. Yes, but it's the only ship I have.

10. A fact.

11. John will soon want money, and I have none to give.

11. ?

12. And the crooked d o c t o r will want money.

12. ?

13. And if Pitman is dishonest, he will want a fortune.

13. ?

"Oh, this seems to be a very one-sided business," wailed Morris. He crumpled the paper up and threw it down on the table in exasperation.

Then, the next moment, he picked the paper up again and smoothed it out. "My position seems to be weakest in its financial aspect. Is there positively no way of raising money? Is there nothing I can sell? I must raise funds! My uncle being dead, the money in the bank is mine or would be mine, if I had managed things more cleverly. I know what any other man would do. Any other man would forge Joseph's signature, although I don't know why I call it forging, since Uncle Joseph's dead, and the money is mine. When I think that Joseph is really dead and I can't prove it, life really does seem cruel."

Cramming his hat upon his head, Morris elbowed his way through the crowd and out of the inn. It was still drizzling. Things certainly couldn't get much worse.

"The more I think about it," Morris reflected, "the more I realize there's nothing to do but find a crooked doctor. That should be simple enough in a city like London. It wouldn't do, of course, to advertise. No, I suppose a fellow must simply spot one in the street and put the proposition to him plainly."

He was nearing home after many hours of wandering through the rain-soaked city. At last, he thrust his key into the lock.

"Not even this house is mine till I can prove that Uncle Joseph's dead," he snarled and slammed the door behind him so that even the windows in the attic rattled.

Night had fallen. Long ago the lamps and the shop windows had begun to glitter down the twisting streets. The hall was pitch-black. As luck would have it, Morris promptly tripped over the statue of Hercules. There was a splintering crash as the statue toppled to the floor.

"Oh, what have I done now?" wailed Morris, and he groped his way to find a candle. "Yes," he mused, as he stood with the light in his hand, "I have mutilated a genuine antique. Don't tell me I owe still another person money!"

And then, from the depths of despair, a pale glimmer of hope. "Wait a minute," he cried aloud. "There's nothing to connect me with this beastly accident. Both Julia and that Gideon fellow have disappeared from view. The moving men have no recollection of the delivery. I'll deny all knowledge of the thing."

A moment later, he stood before the Hercules, an ax under one arm, a sledge hammer under the other. Two hours later, what had once been whole was now no more than a medley of scattered members. Half an hour more and all the debris had been laboriously carted into the kitchen. Morris looked upon the scene of his crime. Yes, he could deny all knowledge of it now. The hall, beyond the fact that it was partly in ruin, betrayed no trace of the passage of Hercules.

Wearily, Morris crept up to bed. His arms and shoulders ached, the palms of his hands burned, and his eyes still smarted from the dust. But even sleep was denied him that night. He counted sheep, he counted money, he counted barrels—to no avail. A tormented Morris witnessed the break of day over London.

The morning, as if in accord with his disastrous fortunes, dawned inclemently. An easterly gale howled in the streets. Sheets of rain sounded against the windowpanes. As Morris dressed, a draft from the fireplace played about his legs.

"I would think," he observed bitterly, "that with all I have to bear, they might have at least given me decent weather."

Julia had not been the most conscientious of housekeepers. The bread was moldy and the milk, left to its own devices, had curdled.

On an empty stomach, Morris sat down at his desk and began his study of the delicate art of forgery. Happily for the investor, forgery is an affair of practice. As Morris sat surrounded by examples of his uncle's signature, and his own incompetence, depression began to grow within him like a weed.

From time to time, the wind wailed in the chimney. From time to time a squall swept over Bloomsbury, pitching the house into such gloom that he was obliged to rise and light the gas. All around him was the chill and disorder of the house. The floor was bare, the sofa was heaped with books and accounts wrapped in a dirty tablecloth. Everything was glazed with a thick film of dust. Yet the true root of his depression lay on the table in the shape of unsuccessful forgeries.

"It's one of the strangest things I've ever heard of," he complained. "It almost seems as if it were a talent that I didn't possess. An accountant would find my attempts laughable. Tracing seems to be the only answer."

He waited until a squall had passed and there came a glimmer of pale daylight. Then he went to the window and traced his uncle's signature. At best, it was a poor copy. "But it must do," he said woefully. "Uncle Joseph is dead anyway." After filling in the check for a couple of hundred pounds, he trotted off to the Bank of England.

There, at the desk where he was accustomed to transact business, and with as much indifference as he could assume, Morris presented the forged check to the big, red-bearded teller. The teller viewed it with surprise. As he turned it over in his hand, his surprise appeared to grow into disapproval. He asked to be excused for a moment and disappeared into the rear offices of the bank. After a lengthy interval, he returned again. At his side, walked a distinguished-looking gentleman.

"Mr. Morris Finsbury, I believe," said the gentleman, peering at Morris through his spectacles.

"That is my name," said Morris, quavering. "Is there anything wrong?"

"Well, the fact is, Mr. Finsbury, you see we are rather surprised to receive this," replied the banker. "There are no funds in your account."

"No funds?" cried Morris. "Why I know myself that there must be £2,800, if there's a penny."

"It was drawn yesterday," said the banker, with finality.

"Drawn!" cried Morris.

"By your uncle himself, sir," continued the banker. "Not only that, but we cashed a check payable to him for £800."

"William Dent Pitman!" cried Morris, staggering back.

"I beg your pardon?" said the banker.

"It's—it's only an expression," stuttered Morris.

"I hope there's nothing wrong, Mr. Finsbury."

"All I can tell you," said Morris with a harsh laugh, "is that the whole thing's impossible. My uncle is vacationing at Browndean."

"Really!" cried the banker. "But the check you just handed us is dated today. How do you account for that?"

"Oh, that was a mistake," said Morris, quickly.

"No doubt, no doubt," said the banker, but he looked at Morris with suspicion.

"And . . . and . . ." sputtered Morris, "even if there were no funds, this is a very trifling sum to overdraw. Our firm—the name of Finsbury—is surely good enough for such a wretched sum as this."

"No doubt," replied the banker, "and if you insist I will take it into consideration. However, Mr. Finsbury, if there had been nothing else, the signature seems hardly all that we could wish."

"That's of no importance," said Morris nervously, "I'll get my uncle to sign another. The fact is," he continued boldly, "my uncle is so ill at present that he was unable to sign this check without assistance, and I fear that my holding the pen for him may have made the difference in the signature."

The banker shot Morris a keen glance, and then turned to the teller.

"Well," he said, "it seems as if we have been victimized by a swindler. Please tell Mr. Finsbury that we shall put detectives on the case at once. As for this check of yours, I regret that, because of the way it was signed, the bank can hardly consider it businesslike," and he returned the check across the counter.

Morris picked it up mechanically. He was thinking of something very different.

"In a case of this kind, who is responsible for the loss?" he asked.

"The bank is most definitely responsible," replied the banker, "and the bank will either recover the money or refund it, you may depend on that."

Morris' face fell.

"I'll tell you what," he said quickly, "you leave this matter entirely in my hands. I've an idea, and detectives," he added appealingly, "are so expensive."

"The bank wouldn't hear of it," retorted the banker. "We stand to lose money. An undiscovered forger is a permanent danger. We shall clear up this matter, Mr. Finsbury. You can set your mind at rest."

"I'll be responsible for the loss," said Morris generously. "I order you to abandon the search."

"I beg your pardon," said the banker, "but we have nothing to do with you in this matter, which is one between your uncle and ourselves. If your uncle agrees, we can visit him in his sickroom . . ."

"Quite impossible!" cried Morris.

"Well, then you see how my hands are tied," said the banker. "The whole affair must be taken to the police at once."

Morris looked at the man blankly and somehow scrambled out of the bank.

"I don't know what they suspect," he thought. "I can't make them out. But it doesn't matter. Everything's over, anyway. The money has been withdrawn. The police are on the scent, in two hours that idiot Pitman will be nabbed, and the whole story of the dead body will appear in the evening papers."

Meanwhile, back at the bank, the teller turned to

his superior with amusement. "That was a highly curious affair, sir."

"Yes, but I think we have given him a fright," said the banker. "We shall hear no more of Morris Finsbury. It was a first attempt, and the Finsburys have dealt with us so long that I was anxious to save the poor man's dignity. But I suppose that there can be no mistake about yesterday? It was old Joseph Finsbury himself?"

"There can be no doubt about that," replied the teller, with a grin. "He explained the principles of banking to me."

"Well, the next time he comes in, ask him to step into my office. He should be warned."

CHAPTER VII
One Barrel Too Many

No. 7 NORFOLK STREET was not a particularly inviting place of residence. Yet it had a character of its own, for here was the home of an artist—a distinguished artist too, highly distinguished by his lack of success.

To the rear of the house was a garden, boasting of a single, battered fountain, a few grimy-looking flowers in pots, two or three newly-planted trees upon which spring had had obviously no effect, and two or three statues, representing satyrs and nymphs in the worst possible style of sculptured art. To one side of the garden stood a wobbly, improvised studio. On its door was a brass plate proudly bearing the inscription "William Dent Pitman, Artist."

All day, it was true, he taught fine arts at a seminary for young ladies, but the evenings at least were his own. He would prolong these evenings far into the night in raptures of creative ecstasy. Mr. Pitman had studied in Paris, and he had studied in Rome, the funds being supplied by a fond parent who went subsequently bankrupt. Although he was never thought to have any talent, it was at one time supposed that he had learned his business. Eighteen years later, even Pitman himself no longer entertained any illusions.

By the dying light of an October day, Pitman viewed his unclaimed treasures with resignation. He was alone in his studio, a dark, weak, harmless, pathetic little man, clad in black, his coat longer than is usual. There was a bald spot on the top of his head, and there were silver hairs at his temples. Poor gentleman, he was no longer young. The passage of time, poverty, and humble ambition thwarted had taken their toll.

In front of him, in the corner by the door, there stood an enormous, solidly-built barrel. No matter where he turned, his eyes remained riveted to the barrel.

"Should I open it? Should I return it? Should I write to Mr. Semitopolis at once?" he wondered. "No, nothing without first consulting Michael Finsbury."

He went to his desk and, after rummaging through the confusion, finally produced his cream-colored notepaper. It was the variety he used when communicating with the proprietors of art schools and the parents of his pupils. He pulled up a chair and began laboriously composing the following letter:

> My dear Michael Finsbury, would it be presuming on your kindness if I asked you to pay me a visit here this evening? I am greatly in need of a lawyer's advice. It is for no trifling matter that I request your valuable assistance, for need I say more than it concerns the welfare of Mr. Semitopolis' statue of Hercules? I write you in great agitation. I have made all possible inquiries and greatly fear that this work of ancient art has been mislaid. I have other problems at present, not unconnected with this one.
>
> Yours in haste, William Dent Pitman

Within the hour, he was ringing the bell of No. 23 King's Road, the private residence of Michael Finsbury.

"No," said the elderly housekeeper who opened the door, "Mr. Finsbury's not in yet. But ye're looking terribly poorly, Mr. Pitman. Have a glass of sherry, sir, to cheer ye up."

"No, I thank you, ma'am," replied the artist. "It is very good of you, but I scarcely feel in the mood for sherry. If you would just give Mr. Finsbury this letter, and tell him to come and see me at his earliest convenience. I shall be in the studio all evening."

He turned once again into the street and walked slowly homeward. A mannequin in a shop window caught his eye, and he stared long and earnestly at the proud, high-born, waxen lady in evening dress. The artist woke in him, in spite of his troubles.

"It's all very well to ridicule the men who make these things," he cried, "but there's a haughty, indefinable something about that figure. They don't teach you that direct appeal in Paris. It's undeniably British. I must wake up, I must aim higher. Yes, I must aim higher!"

All through his afternoon tea, Pitman's imagination dwelt rapturously on art and the artist. No sooner had he swallowed his last crumpet than he hastened with positive exhilaration to his studio.

Not even the sight of the barrel could depress his spirits. He flung himself with rising zest into his work and was recalled to the cares of life only by Michael Finsbury's rattle at the door.

"Well, what's wrong?" said Michael, noting the bright fire in the grate with obvious pleasure. "I suppose you have come to grief somehow."

"There is no expression strong enough," cried the artist. "Mr. Semitopolis' statue has not turned up, and I am afraid that I shall be answerable for the money. For a man of my means, this is no little consideration. But I think nothing of that. What I fear, my dear Michael Finsbury, what I fear is exposure. The Hercules was smuggled out of Italy, under the very noses of the authorities. A thing positively wrong, a thing in which a man of my principles and in my responsible position should have taken no part."

"This sounds like very serious business," said the lawyer. "It will require a great deal of drink."

"In short, I took the liberty of being prepared for you," replied the artist, pointing to a bottle of gin, a lemon, and glasses.

Michael mixed himself a grog, and offered the artist a cigar.

"No, thank you," said Pitman. "I used to be rather partial to them, but the smell is so disagreeable."

"All right," said Michael. "I am comfortable now. Unfold your tale."

At some length, Pitman enumerated his sorrows. He had gone to Waterloo Station today, expecting to receive the Hercules, and had received a barrel instead. Yet the barrel's label was addressed to him in the handwriting of his Italian associate. What was stranger still, a packing case had arrived on the same train, one large enough and heavy enough to contain the Hercules. This packing case had been taken to an untraceable address. The moving men had been drinking and could remember nothing of the delivery. They were discharged at once by the stationmaster, who behaved most properly throughout and was going to make inquiries at Southampton. "In the meantime, what was I to do? I left my address with the stationmaster and brought the barrel home. Remembering the old adage, I decided not to open it except in the presence of my lawyer."

"Is that all?" asked Michael. "I don't see any cause for worry. The Hercules has probably been held up in the mails. You'll most likely receive it in a day or two. As for the barrel, perhaps it's a token of appreciation from one of your young ladies. Maybe it's oysters."

"Oh, don't speak so loud!" cried the little artist. "It would cost me my job if I were heard speaking lightly of the young ladies, and besides, why oysters from Italy, and why should they come to me addressed in my Italian associate's hand?"

"Well, let's have a look at it," said Michael. "Bring it here towards the light."

The two men rolled the barrel from the corner, and stood it on end before the fire.

"It's certainly heavy enough to be osyters," said Michael, with a laugh.

"Shall we open it at once?" asked Pitman, who had grown decidedly cheerful under the combined effects of company and gin. Without waiting for a reply, the artist stripped to the waist, and with a chisel in one hand and a hammer in the other, struck the first blow of the evening.

"That's the style, Pitman!" cried Michael. "There's fire for your money! It may be a romantic visit from one of the young ladies. A sort of Cleopatra act. Be careful and don't bash in Cleopatra's head."

The sight of Pitman's eagerness was infectious. The lawyer could sit still no longer. Tossing his cigar into the fire, he snatched the hammer from the hands of the artist. Soon, the sweat formed beads upon his brow. His stylish trousers were streaked with iron rust, and the state of his hammer testified to misdirected energies.

A barrel is not an easy thing to open, even when one goes about it in the right way. When one goes about it wrongly, the whole structure must be reduced to splinters. This was the course pursued by the artist and the lawyer. Presently the last hoop had been removed, and what had once been a barrel was no more than a confused heap of broken and distorted boards.

In the midst of the pile, a certain dismal something, swathed in blankets, remained upright for an instant, and then toppled to one side and collapsed heavily before the fire. As the thing hit the floor, a pair of spectacles rolled toward the screaming Pitman.

"Hold your tongue!" cried Michael. He dashed for the front door and locked it. Then, with a pale face and trembling hands, he drew near, pulled aside a corner of the blanket, and recoiled, shuddering.

There was a long silence in the studio.

"Now, tell me," said Michael, in a low voice, "did you have any hand in it?" and he pointed to the body.

The artist could only utter broken and disjointed sounds.

Michael poured some gin into a glass. "Drink that," he ordered. "Don't be afraid of me. I'm your friend through thick and thin."

"I swear before God," Pitman said, "this is yet another mystery to me. In my worst moments, I would never have dreamed of such a thing. I would not lay a finger on a bothersome mosquito."

"Well, that's settled," said Michael, with a sigh of relief. "I believe you, old boy." He shook the artist warmly by the hand. "I thought for a moment," he added, with a ghastly smile, "I thought for a moment that you might have done away with Mr. Semitopolis."

"It would make no difference if I had," groaned Pitman. "Everything's over now. The handwriting is on the wall."

"To begin with," said Michael, "let's get the body out of sight. To be quite plain with you, Pitman, I don't like your friend's appearance. Where can we put it?"

"You might put it in the closet over there—if you could bear to touch it," replied the artist.

"Somebody has to do it, Pitman," said the lawyer. "You go over to the table, turn your back, and mix me a grog. That's a fair division of labor."

A moment later, the closet door was shut with a bang.

"There," said Michael, "that's more cosy. You can turn now, Pitman. Is this the grog? My word, it's a lemonade!"

"Oh, Michael, what are we to do with the body?" wailed the artist.

"Do with it?" repeated Michael. "Bury it in your garden, and erect one of your own statues for a monument. Here, put some gin in this."

"I beg of you, Michael Finsbury, do not trifle with my misery," cried Pitman. "You see before you a man who has been eminently respectable all his life. Even in this solemn hour, I can lay my hand upon my heart without a blush. Except for the smuggling of the Hercules, my life has been without a blemish. I never feared the light. But now . . ."

"Cheer up, old boy," said Michael. "I assure you it's the sort of thing that could happen to any one. If you're perfectly sure you had no hand in it . . ."

"What words am I to find . . ." began Pitman.

"Oh, I'll do that part of it," interrupted Michael, "you have no experience. But since you know nothing of the crime, since the 'party in the closet' is neither your father, nor your brother, nor your creditor, nor your mother-in-law . . ."

"Oh, my dear Michael Finsbury!" interjected Pitman, horrified.

"Since, in short," continued the lawyer, "you had no possible interest in the crime, we have a perfectly free field before us and a safe game to play. Indeed, the problem is really entertaining. Don't worry, I mean to pull you through. Let's see. It's been a long time since I have had what I call a genuine holiday. Tomorrow, I'll send an excuse to my office."

"In the meantime, to return to the immediate question of the body . . ." ventured Pitman.

"If you won't take the shortcut and bury it in your garden, we must find someone who will bury it in his. We must place the affair in the hands of someone of fewer scruples and more resources."

"A private detective, perhaps?" suggested Pitman.

"There are times when you fill me with pity," replied the lawyer. "By the way, Pitman, I have always regretted that you have no piano in this studio of yours. Even if you don't play yourself, your friends might like to entertain themselves with a little music when they come to call."

"I shall get one at once if you like," said Pitman nervously, anxious to please. "I play the fiddle a little myself."

"I know you do," said Michael, "but what's the fiddle, especially the way you play it? Since it's too late for you to buy a piano, I'll give you mine."

"Thank you," said the artist blankly. "You will give me yours? It's really too good of you."

"Yes, I'll give you mine," continued Michael, "for the inspector of police to play on while his men are digging up your garden."

Pitman stared at him in pained amazement.

"No, I'm not insane," said Michael. "I'm playful, that's all. Listen, Pitman, I mean to profit from the refreshing fact that we are really and truly innocent. Nothing but the presence of the body in the closet connects us with the crime. Once we get rid of it, no matter how, there is no possible clue to trace us by. Well, I'll give you my piano. We'll bring it around tonight. Tomorrow we'll rip the interior out of it, deposit our friend inside, plump the whole business on a cart, and bring it to the home of an acquaintance of mine. I once did a favor for him, and he gave me all he had, including the key to his house. It's there that I propose to leave the piano and, shall we say, Cleopatra?"

"It seems like a wild scheme," said Pitman. "What will become of your acquaintance?"

"It will do him good," said Michael cheerfully. "It's just what he needs."

"But he might become involved in a murder charge," gulped Pitman.

"Well, he'll be in the same position we are," replied Michael. "He's innocent, you see. What hangs people, my dear Pitman, is the unfortunate circumstance of guilt."

"I'm not convinced. Wouldn't it be safer just to send for the police?" pleaded Pitman.

"Do you want a scandal on your hands? What would they say at the seminary for young ladies?"

"It would mean my discharge," admitted Pitman. "I can't deny that."

"And besides," said Michael, "I want some fun for my money."

"Is that the proper spirit?" cried Pitman.

"Oh, I only said that to cheer you up," replied Michael. "There's nothing more to discuss. If you're going to follow my advice, let's bring the piano here at once. If you prefer, I'll leave and let you deal with the whole thing according to your better judgment."

"You know perfectly well that I depend on you entirely," wailed Pitman. "But oh, what a night is before me!"

An hour later, Michael's piano, a monumentous Broadwood grand, was deposited in Pitman's studio.

CHAPTER VIII

The Devil's Advocate

PUNCTUALLY AT EIGHT O'CLOCK the next morning, Michael Finsbury rattled on the studio door. He found the artist sadly altered for the worse. His eyes were bloodshot, his complexion chalky. He had a certain blank expression about the face which clearly indicated shock.

"Here I am, William Dent Pitman!" Michael cried, and drawing from his pocket two little wisps of reddish hair, he held them to his cheeks like whiskers and danced about the studio. The lawyer was usually dressed in the height of fashion, but today he had fallen altogether from these heights. He wore a flannel shirt of washed-out tartan, a suit of reddish tweeds, a hat of purple felt, and his feet were shod with rugged walking boots.

Pitman laughed sadly. "I would never have known you," he said.

"Nor were you intended to," replied Michael, replacing his false whiskers in his pocket. "Now we must find a disguise for you."

"Disguise!" cried the artist. "Must I really disguise myself? Has it come to that?"

"My dear friend," cried Michael, "what is life without the pleasures of disguise? I know it's unprofessional, but that's the way it has to be. We have to leave a false impression on the minds of many persons, and in particular on the mind of Mr. Gideon Forsyth, the young gentleman who offered me the key to his house. He might have the bad taste to be at home."

"And if he's at home?" faltered Pitman. "That would be the end of it all."

"It won't matter," replied Michael flippantly. "Let me see your clothes, and I'll make a new man of you in a jiffy."

Once in the bedroom, Michael examined Pitman's poor and scanty wardrobe with a humorous eye. He picked out a short jacket of black alpaca and added a pair of summer trousers. Then, with the garments in his hand, he scrutinized the artist closely.

"I don't like that vest," he said. "Have you nothing else?"

Pitman pondered for a moment and then suggested brightly, "I have a low-necked shirt that I used to wear in Paris as a student. It's rather loud."

"Just the thing!" exclaimed Michael. "You'll look perfectly beastly. Now, wait here for three quarters of an hour. After that you can rejoin me on the field of glory."

A moment later, Michael made a dash for the studio. An easterly gale tormented the sky. The wind blew shrilly among the statues in the garden and drove the rain upon the skylight in the studio. At about the same time as Morris attacked the hundredth version of Uncle Joseph's signature in Bloomsbury, Michael began to rip the wires out of his Broadwood piano.

Precisely three quarters of an hour later, Pitman arrived in the studio. The short trip from the main house had left him soaking wet. He viewed the open closet door, the untenanted closet, and the discreetly shut piano with foreboding.

"Yes, indeed. It's a heavy instrument," said Michael, turning to examine Pitman's disguise. "You must shave off that beard of yours."

"My beard!" cried Pitman. "I cannot shave off my beard. I cannot tamper with my appearance. The principal of the seminary would object. They have very strong views on the appearance of the staff. Young ladies are considered so romantic. My beard was regarded with favor at the school. It was regarded," said the artist, with hesitation, "it was regarded as unbecoming."

"You can let it grow again," replied Michael, "and then you'll be so ugly that they'll raise your salary."

"But I don't want to look ugly," cried Pitman.

"Don't be a fool," said Michael, who hated beards and was delighted to destroy one. "Off with it like a man!"

"Of course, if you insist," said Pitman. He brought some hot water from the kitchen, and placing a glass upon his easel, first clipped his beard with scissors and then shaved his chin. He could not deny, as he regarded the result, that his last claims to manhood had been sacrificed, but Michael seemed delighted.

"You're a new man!" he cried.

Pitman did not reply, but continued to gaze disconsolately at his reflection in the mirror.

"Well, I must say you're the poorest companion. And just when I was enjoying myself. We might as well begin the business at hand. Come to think of it," Michael gasped in dismay, "I've made an abominable error. You should have ordered the cart before you were disguised. Why, Pitman, what use are you? Why couldn't you have reminded me of that?"

"I never even knew there was a cart to be ordered," said the artist. "But I can take off the disguise again," he added eagerly.

"You would find it rather a bother to put on your beard," said Michael, drily. "No, it's a false step. It's the sort of thing that hangs people," he continued cheerfully, as he sipped some brandy, "and it can't be retraced now. Go make all the arrangements. Have the piano taken from here as soon as possible. It's to be carted to Victoria Station and stored there until called for in the name of Brown. Don't make any mistakes now, unless you want us both hanged."

"I wish," said Pitman, "for my sake, I wish you wouldn't talk so much of hanging."

"Talking about it is nothing, my boy!" replied Michael. "Off with you, and don't forget to pay for everything beforehand."

Left to himself, the lawyer turned his attention exclusively to the consumption of brandy. His spirits rose. At that moment, the spectacles flashed into his mind. He put them on, and fell in love with the effect. "Just what I needed," he said, and he began to practice different styles of walking before the mirror. In the midst of his walk of an Australian colonist revisiting the scenes of childhood, his eye lighted on the piano. Michael opened it and ran his fingers over the soundless keys. "Fine instrument. A full, rich tone," he decided and he pulled up a chair.

When Pitman returned to the studio, he was appalled to see the lawyer performing on the silent grand.

"Forgive me, but I fear you have been drinking," wailed the artist.

Michael, without rising, turned a flushed face, encircled with a bush of red whiskers, and punctuated with the spectacles, upon him. "Capriccio in B-flat on the departure of a friend," he proclaimed, continuing his noiseless rendition.

Indignation awoke in Pitman's mind. "Those spectacles were to be mine," he cried. "They are an essential part of my disguise."

"I am going to wear them myself," replied Michael. "A lot of suspicion would be aroused if we both wore spectacles."

"Oh, well," said Pitman, "I had counted on them, but if you insist. At any rate, the cart has arrived."

While the men were at work, Michael hid in the closet among the debris of the barrel and the wires of the piano. As soon as the coast was clear, the pair dashed from the house, jumped into a carriage, and were driven rapidly toward the center of town.

It was still cold and raw. The rain pelted their faces, but Michael refused to raise the windows. In high spirits, he pointed out the sights of London as they drove along. "My dear fellow," he said, "you seem to know nothing of your native city. Suppose we visited the Tower? No? Well, perhaps it's a trifle out of our way. Here, cabby, drive around Trafalgar Square!" He insisted on pulling to a halt while he criticized the statues and gave the artist many curious details on the lives of the celebrated men they represented.

It would be difficult to express what Pitman suffered in the carriage: cold, wet terror, a basic distrust in the whole wild scheme, a bitter sense of the decline and fall involved in the deprivation of his beard.

At last, the carriage drew to a halt. Pitman viewed the restaurant with obvious relief. A second and still greater relief was, hearing Michael request a private room. As they climbed the stairs, Pitman did not fail to notice that the place was half empty. It was a blessed thought that no one connected with the seminary for young ladies would frequent such an establishment.

The waiter led them into a small, bare room with a single table, a sofa, and a dying fire in the grate. Michael promptly called for more coals and a couple of brandies.

"Oh, no," said Pitman, "no more to drink."

"I don't know about you," said Michael plaintively, "but I need something to bolster my spirits."

Pitman looked around in dismay. Here he was, ridiculously shorn, absurdly disguised, and in the company of a drunken man in spectacles. What would his principal think, if he could see him? What if he knew about his tragic and deceitful errand?

He was aroused from his meditations by the entrance of the waiter with the brandies. Michael took one and passed the other to his friend.

Pitman waved it from him with his hand. "Don't let me lose all self-respect," he said.

"Anything to oblige a friend," replied Michael. "But I'm not going to drink alone. Here," he added to the waiter, "you take it. To the health of Gideon Forsyth," he said, touching glasses.

"To the health of Gideon Forsyth," repeated the waiter, ceremoniously.

"Have another?" said Michael. "I never saw a man drink faster. It restores one's confidence in the human race."

But the waiter excused himself politely and began to bring in lunch.

Michael ate heartily. As for the artist, he was far too uneasy to eat.

"Enough of this," proclaimed Michael, downing a brandy. "On to the business at hand. You can't go into this sort of thing too thoroughly, Pitman. The whole secret is preparation. We have already disguised our appearances. Now, we must disguise our identities. Listen carefully. I am an Australian. My name is John Dickson. You will be relieved to hear that I am rich, sir, very rich. I'd tell you my life's story, only I seem to have forgotten it."

"Perhaps I'm stupid . . ." began Pitman.

"That's it!" cried Michael. "Very stupid. But you're rich too, richer than I am. I thought that you'd enjoy it, Pitman, so I've arranged that you were to be literally wallowing in wealth. But then, on the other hand, you're an American. And the worst of it is that you're called Ezra Thomas. Now, tell me who we are."

The unfortunate Pitman was cross-examined until he knew all the facts by heart.

"There!" cried Michael. "The die is cast!"

"But I don't understand," wailed Pitman.

"Oh, you'll understand soon enough," said Michael, rising.

"There doesn't seem any story to it," said the artist.

"We can invent one as we go along," replied the lawyer.

"But I can't invent," protested Pitman. "All my life, I never could invent anything."

"You'll find you have to," said Michael, and he began calling for the waiter.

Of course, he is very clever, but can I trust him in such a state? Pitman asked himself.

Once again in the carriage, the artist summoned his courage. "Don't you think," he faltered, "it would be wiser, all things considered, just to drop the whole business?"

"Put off till tomorrow what can be done today?" cried Michael, with indignation. "I never heard of such a thing! Cheer up, things can't get much worse, my lion-hearted friend!"

At Victoria Station, they inquired for Mr. Brown's piano and contracted for a cart. While the cart was being readied, Michael toppled against the wall and fell into a gentle slumber. Pitman found himself left to his own resources in the midst of several staring loafers.

"Rough day, sir," observed one.

"Yes, it is rather a rough day," agreed the artist. Then, feeling that he should change the conversation, added, "My friend is an Australian; he is very impulsive."

"An Australian?" said another. "I've a brother in Melbourne. Does your friend come from there?"

"No, not exactly," replied Pitman, whose idea of Australian geography was a little vague. "He lives far inland, and is very rich."

The loafers gazed with great respect upon the slumbering Michael.

"Well," asserted the second speaker, "Australia is a mighty big place. Do you come from there, too?"

"No, I do not," said Pitman. "I do not, and I don't want to either," he added irritably. Then, feeling at the end of his patience, he pounced upon Michael and shook him violently.

"Hey," said the lawyer, "what's wrong?"

"The cart is nearly ready," said Pitman sternly. "I will not allow you to sleep."

"All right, old man, no offense intended," replied Michael, yawning. "A little sleep never did anybody any harm. I feel comparatively sober now. But what's all the hurry?" he added, looking around him glassily. "I don't see the cart, and I've forgotten where we left the piano."

By the most blessed circumstance, at that moment a porter appeared with the cart in tow.

"You'll drive, of course," ordered Michael, as he clambered on the vehicle.

"I drive!" cried Pitman. "I can't drive. I never did such a thing in my life."

"Very well," replied Michael. "As you like. Anything to oblige a friend."

Mr. Brown's piano was deposited, after a small struggle, on board.

"Well, sir," said the porter, as he mentally added up a handful of loose silver, "that's a mighty heavy piano."

"It's the richness of the tone," said Michael as he drove away.

It was but a little distance in the rain, which now fell thickly, and the cart reached Gideon Forsyth's house without disaster. There, in a deserted alley, Michael drew up the horses and the pair set forth on foot for the scene of their adventure. For the first time, Michael showed signs of uneasiness.

"Are my whiskers all right?" he asked. "I'd hate to be spotted."

"They are perfectly in place," replied Pitman. "How's my disguise?"

"Oh, nobody could recognize you without your beard," said Michael. "All you have to do is remember to speak slowly. You speak through your nose already."

"I only hope the young man won't be at home," sighed Pitman.

"And I only hope he'll be alone," said Michael.

When they finally knocked at the door, Gideon admitted them in person to a room warmed by a small fire in the grate. The walls were lined with leather-covered legal books, although the desk was conspicuously bare. In one corner of the blotter stood a container of well-sharpened pencils.

"Mr. Forsyth, I believe?" inquired Michael. "We have come to trouble you with a piece of business. I fear it's scarcely professional to call without an appointment, but time flies and we are sorely in need of legal advice."

"May I inquire, gentlemen," asked Gideon, "to whom I am indebted for a recommendation?"

"You may inquire," replied Michael, taking a chair and motioning Pitman to do the same, "but I was instructed not to tell you until the thing was done."

"My uncle Hugh, no doubt," decided Gideon.

"My name is John Dickson," continued Michael, "a pretty well-known name in Ballarat. My friend here is Mr. Ezra Thomas, of the United States of America, a wealthy manufacturer."

"Stop one moment while I make a note of that," said Gideon, with a professional air.

"Perhaps you wouldn't mind my smoking a cigar?" asked Michael. His thoughts had begun to run together and he hoped a cigar would clear his head.

"Oh, certainly," cried Gideon blandly. "Try one of mine. I can confidently recommend them." And he handed the box to his client.

"I hope I am making myself perfectly clear," said Michael.

"Oh, certainly," replied the affable Gideon. "Please take your time. I can give you," he added, thoughtfully consulting his watch, "I can give you the whole afternoon."

"The business that brings us here," began Michael, "is frightfully delicate. That I can tell you. My friend Mr. Thomas, a wealthy manufacturer of Broadwood pianos, combines many, many, many professions. Mr.

Thomas' cotton mills are one of the sights of Tallahassee. Mr. Thomas' tobacco plantations are the pride of Richmond. In short, Mr. Forsyth, he's one of my oldest friends, and I lay his case before you with emotion."

Gideon looked at the object of all this discussion and was agreeably impressed by his open, although nervous, manner. What a people are these Americans! he thought. Look at this timid, weedy, simple little man, and think of him wielding and directing interests so extended and seemingly incongruous! "But shouldn't we," he observed aloud, "get down to facts?"

"You're a man of business, I see!" cried Michael. "It's a case of blackmail."

The unhappy Pitman was so unprepared for this turn of events that he could scarcely suppress a cry.

"Dear me," said Gideon, "blackmail can be a dirty business. Tell me everything you know. If you want my assistance, conceal nothing."

"*You* tell him," said Michael, feeling, apparently, that he had done his share. "My friend will tell you all about it," he added to Gideon, with a yawn.

Pitman gazed blankly about the room. Rage and despair seethed within him. Thoughts of flight, thoughts even of suicide, passed through his head. Gideon waited patiently while the artist groped in vain for any form of words, however insignificant.

"Yes, it's a case of blackmail," he said at last, in a low voice. Then, in a desperate quest for inspiration, he made a cluth at his beard. His fingers closed upon the unfamiliar smoothness of a shaven chin, and in that moment hope and courage fled forever. He shook Michael roughly. "Wake up!" he cried irritably. "I can't do it, you know I can't."

"You must excuse my friend," said Michael. "He has no talent for narration. The case is really very simple. My friend wrote a series of compromising letters to a young woman. If these letters are produced in court, sir, my friend's reputation is gone."

"Am I to understand. . ." began Gideon.

"My dear sir," said Michael, "it isn't possible to understand unless you saw the letters."

"This is a painful case," said Gideon, glancing at the culprit with pity.

"But that's only the beginning," wailed Michael. "I wish with all my heart I could say that my friend's hands were clean. He has no excuse, for he was engaged at the time, and is still engaged, to the belle of Ga."

" 'Ga'?" repeated Gideon.

"An abbreviation in current use," explained Michael. "*Ga* stands for Georgia, in the same way as *Co* stands for Company."

"Yes, yes," agreed Gideon eagerly.

"You can see for yourself, sir, how this unhappy

person is in need of a good lawyer. My friend has money, and he's not a miser. He could write a check tomorrow for £100,000. Now go find the young lady in question and threaten, bribe, or both, until you get the letters. If you can't, my friend must go to court and exposure is always a very disagreeable affair."

"To what figure may I go?" asked Gideon.

"Perhaps £5,000 would be enough for today," replied Michael. "Don't let us detain you any longer. Time is flying. There are plenty of trains to Hampton Court. Here is a five-pound note for current expenses and here is the address." He began to write, paused, tore up the paper, and put the pieces in his pocket. "I will dictate," he said. "My writing is so illegible. The name is Selena Tarnow of Shady Villa, Hampton Court."

"And now, gentlemen, where shall I communicate with you?" asked Gideon.

"The Royal Hotel," replied Michael. "Till tonight, then."

"Till tonight!" cried Gideon. "I suppose that I can call at any hour?"

"Any hour, any hour," murmured Michael, backing out the door with the artist in tow. "Hey!" he cried, as soon as they were in the street. "What's wrong with the long-suffering Pitman?"

"You had no right to speak of me as you did. Your language was indecent and you have wounded me deeply."

"I never said a word about you," replied Michael. "I spoke of Mr. Ezra Thomas, and please remember that there's no such person."

"It's just as hard to take," mumbled Pitman.

They had reached the alley, and the uncovered piano, upright on its cart, glistened in the rain. The last battle of the campaign opened.

Gideon had scarcely claimed his seat in the train for Hampton Court, before the Broadwood grand was deposited in the middle of his apartment. Had he known what was taking place in his absence, he might have harbored less kindly feelings for his new clients.

"And now," said Michael, thumping the exhausted Pitman on the back, "one more precaution. We must leave the key to the piano in an obvious place."

"Poor young man," said Pitman, as they closed the door to Gideon's apartment. "That reminds me, Michael, I'd like to apologize for speaking the way I did. I had no right to resent expressions, wounding as they were, which were in no sense directed personally at me."

"That's all right," cried Michael, climbing on the cart. "Not a word more, Pitman. No self-respecting man can stand by and hear his *alias* insulted."

The rain had stopped, the body had been disposed of, and the friends were reconciled. The ride to Victoria Station was a lighthearted occasion. When the pair had returned the cart, unchallenged and even unsuspected, Pitman drew a deep breath of joy.

"Now," he cried happily, "we can go home."

"Pitman," said Michael, stopping short, "your recklessness fills me with concern. We have been wet the greater part of the day, and you propose, in cold blood, to go home! No, my good friend, it's unthinkable!"

And taking the artist firmly by the arm, Michael led him straight to the nearest public inn.

CHAPTER IX

A Family Reunion

✦✦✦✦✦✦✦✦✦✦✦✦✦✦✦

THE HOUSE ON KING'S ROAD was kept very quiet. When Michael entertained guests, it was at the local lawyer's club; the door of his private residence remained closed against his friends. The upper floor, which was sunny, was set apart for his father, Masterson. The elder Finsbury had been ailing, and his right to privacy was respected by all the occupants of the house.

The dining room was the center of Michael's life. It was here in this pleasant room, sheltered from the curiosity of King's Road by drawn blinds, that Michael sat down to dinner after his adventures with Pitman. A wiry old lady, with very bright eyes, waited upon the lawyer's needs. She had been with the Finsburys a long time, and as the years passed it became increasingly unclear who was servant and who was master.

"I think, Teena, I'll have a brandy and soda," said Michael fearfully, like a man not certain of obedience.

"Nothing doing, Mr. Michael," was the prompt reply. "Water will do."

"Very well, Teena, I guess you know best," sighed Michael. "Very tiring day at the office, though."

"What?" exclaimed Teena. "You never were near the office! Take care! Don't break my crystal!" she added.

"And how is my father?" asked Michael.

"Oh, just the same, Mr. Michael, just the way he'll be till the end, worthy man!" Teena replied. "But you'll not be the first that's asked me that question today."

"No?" said the lawyer. "Who else?"

"A friend of yours," said Teena grimly. "Mr. Morris."

"Morris! What was he doing here?" cried Michael.

"Wanting to see him," replied the housekeeper, pointing toward the upper floor. "He tried to bribe me, Mr. Michael. Bribe *me*," she repeated scornfully. "Mr. Morris is no gentleman."

"I bet he didn't offer much," teased Michael.

"He was sent about his business straightway," said Teena gallantly. "He'll not come here again in a hurry."

"He must not see my father!" cried Michael. "I'm not going to have any public exhibition to a little beast like him."

"No fear of my letting him," replied the housekeeper. "But the best of the joke is that he thinks your father's dead, and you're keeping it a secret."

Michael whistled. "I'll make him dance for that."

"Couldn't you get the law after him?" suggested Teena.

"No, I don't think I could," replied Michael. "Listen Teena, give me a bit of brandy and soda, there's a good soul." Tenna's face grew stern. "Well then," said the lawyer fretfully, "I won't eat any more dinner."

"Suit yourself, Mr. Michael," said the housekeeper, as she began clearing the table.

"I do wish Teena weren't such a faithful servant," sighed the lawyer, closing the front door of No. 23, King's Road behind him.

The rain had stopped falling. It was a clear night,

and the town glittered with street lamps. "Things are looking up," thought Michael to himself, as he walked along listening to the million footfalls of the city.

Near the end of King's Road, he remembered his brandy and soda and entered a public inn. The place was packed, but the great attraction was a little old man in a black suit, which was obviously a recent purchase. On the marble table in front of him, beside a sandwich and a glass of beer, there lay a battered hunting cap. The man's hand fluttered with oratorical gestures; his voice boomed across the crowded room. The barmaid, four waiters, and half-a-dozen of the chronically unemployed stood spellbound.

"I have examined all the theatres in London," he was saying, "and after measuring the principal entrances, have come to the conclusion that they are ridiculously disproportionate to the requirements of their audiences. The doors opened the wrong way. What's more, they were frequently locked during the performance, even when the auditorium was literally thronged with English people. You have probably not had my opportunities of comparing distant lands, but I can assure that this sort of thing has long been recognized as a mark of aristocratic government. Do you suppose, in a country really self-governed, that such abuses should exist? Your own intelligence, however uncultivated, tells you they could not!"

"Hey, old gentleman, is it really you?" said Michael, laying his hand upon the speechmaker's shoulder.

The man spun around with alarm. He was indeed Mr. Joseph Finsbury.

"You, Michael!" he cried. "There's no one with you, is there?"

"No," replied Michael, ordering a brandy and soda, "there's no one with me. Whom do you expect?"

"I was afraid it might be Morris or John," said the old gentleman with relief.

"What the devil would I be doing with Morris or John?" cried the nephew.

"Well, I see your point," said Joseph. "I believe I can trust you. You'll stand by me."

"I don't know what you mean," said Michael.

"I'll explain everything later," said Joseph, shaking his nephew by the hand.

"All right," agreed Michael. "This is my treat, Uncle Joseph. What will you have?"

"In that case," replied the old gentleman hurriedly, "I'd like another sandwich. I dare say I surprise you," he continued, "with my presence in a public inn, but the fact is that one must accommodate one's self to the customs of the land. In London, for example, a man can live luxuriously on an annual salary of fourteen pounds, twelve shillings."

"Yes, I know," said Michael, "but that's that's not including food, clothes, or lodging. The whole thing, with cigars and occasional sprees, costs me over seven hundred a year."

But this was Michael's last interruption. He listened in good-humored silence to the remainder of his uncle's lecture, which speedily turned to political reform, then to the scientific theory behind the compass, and finally to a general survey of a dying race of mammals. With that, the sandwich having been consumed, the pair set forth along King's Road.

"Michael," said his uncle, "the reason that I am here is because I cannot endure those nephews of mine. I find them intolerable."

"I'm sure you do," agreed Michael, "I never could stand them for a moment."

"They wouldn't let me speak," continued Joseph bitterly. "I was never allowed to get a word in edgewise. I was shut up at once with some impertinent remark. My pencil allowance was miserly, when I wished to make notes of the most absorbing interest. The daily newspaper was guarded from me like a young baby from a gorilla. You know me, Michael. I live for my calculations. I live for my manifold and ever-changing views on life. Pens and papers are as important to me as food and drink. My life had grown quite intolerable when, in the confusion of that fortunate railway crash at Browndean, I made my escape. Morris and John must think me dead and are trying to hide the fact so as not to lose the tontine. They had no real interest in me, but for that tontine."

"I'll tell you what," said Michael, "come and stay with me."

"Michael," said the old gentleman, "it's very kind of you, but you scarcely understand my position. There are some financial complications. As my nephews' guardian, my efforts were not altogether blessed. I had the lack of foresight to invest their fortune unwisely. Yes, I am absolutely in the power of that vile fellow, Morris."

"How do you happen to have any money at all?" asked Michael. "Don't treat me like a stranger, Uncle Joseph. I know all about the trust and the mess you made of it, and the arrangement you were forced to strike with Morris."

Joseph narrated his dealings with the bank.

"Now you've put your foot in it!" cried Michael. "You had no right to do what you did."

"The whole thing is mine, Michael," protested Joseph. "I founded and nursed that leather business on my own principles."

"That's all very fine," said the lawyer, "but you were forced to transfer everything to Morris. Even then your position was extremely shaky. But this, my dear uncle, means prison."

"Surely the law cannot be so unjust!" cried Joseph.

"And the cream of the thing," interrupted Michael, with a sudden shout of laughter, "the cream of the thing is that you've bankrupted the leather business! I must say, Uncle Joseph, you have strange ideas of law, but I like your taste in humor."

"I see nothing to laugh at," muttered Joseph darkly.

"Has Morris any power to sign for the firm?" asked Michael.

"No one but myself," replied Joseph.

"Oh, poor devil of a Morris!" cried the lawyer in delight. "And he still pretends to have you safely locked away! Oh, Morris, fate has delivered you into my hands! Let me see, Uncle Joseph, what do you suppose the leather business is worth?"

"It was worth a £100,00" said Joseph bitterly, "when it was in my hands. But then that Scot led it to the brink of financial ruin, and then came Morris, who is perfectly incompetent. It's hardly a profit-making enterprise any more."

"I shall turn my attention to the leather trade," said Michael, with decision.

"I advise you not to," said Joseph. "There is nothing in the whole field of commerce more surprising than the fluctuations of the leather market. Its sensitiveness may be described as morbid."

"And now, Uncle Joseph, what have you done with all that money?" asked the lawyer.

"I deposited it in a bank and withdrew twenty pounds," answered Joseph Finsburg promptly. "Why?"

"Very well," said Michael. "Tomorrow I shall send down a clerk with a check for a hundred pounds. He'll withdraw the original sum and return it to the Bank of England, with some sort of explanation which I will try to invent for you. That will clear you for the moment, and as Morris can't touch a penny of it without forgery, it will do no harm to my little scheme."

"But how will I live without any money?" asked Joseph.

"Didn't you listen?" retorted Michael. "I'm going to send along a check for a hundred pounds. That leaves you eighty to live on. When you've spent the eighty, ask me for more."

"I would rather not be beholden to you," said Joseph, with dignity. "I would rather live on my own money, since I have it."

Michael grasped his arm. "Will nothing make you

understand," he cried, "that I am trying to save you from prison?"

His earnestness staggered the old man. "I must turn my attention to law," he said. "It will be a new field, for although I understand, of course, its general principles, I have never really applied my mind to the details. But you may be right, and of course at my age any long term of imprisonment would be highly prejudicial. But, my dear nephew, I have no claim on you. You're not obliged to support me."

"That's all right," said Michael. "I'll probably get it out of the leather business."

Michael took down the old gentleman's address, and left him at the corner of a street.

"What a funny thing life is," the lawyer mused. "I seem condemned to be the instrument of fate. Let's see, what have I done today? Disposed of a dead body, saved Pitman, saved my Uncle Joseph, brought Gideon clients, and consumed a formidable lot of brandy. I'll top the day off with a visit to my cousins. Tomorrow, I can turn my attention to the leather trade. Tonight, I'll just give old Morris a good scare."

About a quarter of an hour later, Michael rapped at the door of No. 16 John Street.

It was promptly opened by Morris.

"Oh, it's you, Michael," he said, carefully blocking the narrow entrance. "It's very late."

Without a word, Michael grasped Morris warmly by the hand, obtained a footing in the hall, and marched into the dining room.

"Where's my Uncle Joseph?" demanded Michael, sitting down in the most comfortable chair.

"He's not been very well lately," replied Morris. "John is caring for him at Browndean. I am alone, as you see."

Michael smiled to himself. "I want to see him for a special reason," he said.

"You can't expect to see my uncle when you won't let me see your father, Masterson," retorted Morris.

"My father is my father," said Michael, "but Joseph is just as much my uncle as he's yours. You have no right to conceal him."

"I do no such thing," said Morris doggedly. "He is not well. As a matter of fact, he is dangerously ill, and nobody can see him."

"I'll tell you what, then," said Michael. "I'll make a clean breast of it. I have come to compromise. Why not have the tontine while we're still young."

Morris turned as pale as death, and then a wave of wrath against the injustice of man's destiny swept over him. "What do you mean?" he cried. "It's too late now. I have my pride. Put that in your pipe and smoke it."

"You say your uncle is dangerously ill, and you won't compromise? There's something very fishy about that."

"What do you mean?" cried Morris hoarsely.

"I only say it's fishy," replied Michael.

"Are you trying to insinuate something?" cried Morris angrily.

"Insinuate?" repeated Michael. "Come on now, don't split hairs. Let us drown our differences in a bottle, like the two kinsmen we are."

"Well," said Morris nervously, "it has been a long time since we've had an evening together. Excuse me one moment while I fetch a bottle from the cellar."

Morris left the room without a word. His quick mind had perceived his advantage. Michael was playing into his hand. "One bottle?" he thought. "By George, I'll give him two! This is not the time for economy. Once the beast is drunk, I'll wring his secret out of him."

Morris returned with a bottle under each arm. He filled their glasses, crying gaily, "I drink to you, cousin!"

Michael emptied his glass, filled it again, and returned to his chair, carrying the bottle along with him.

"The spoils of war!" he said heartily. "The weakest goes to the wall. Look lively, Morris. Oh, but you're a deep one."

"What makes you think I'm deep?" asked Morris, with a pleased air.

"Because you won't compromise," replied the lawyer. "You're a deep dog, Morris, a very deep dog."

"Well, *you* wouldn't compromise before, you know," said Morris, wringing his hands.

"I wonder why *I* wouldn't compromise? I wonder why *you* won't? I wonder why we think the other wouldn't?" asked Michael.

"What do you think my reasons are?"

Michael looked at his cousin and winked. "Next thing, you'll ask me to help you out of the mess you're in. Must be a dreadful muddle for a young orphan of forty. The leather trade and all!"

"I'm not sure I know what you mean," said Morris.

"Not sure I know myself," said Michael. "This is exc'lent wine, sir. Only thing wrong—valuable uncle disappeared. Now what I want to know is where's valuable uncle?"

"I've already told you. He's at Browndean," answered Morris, wiping his hand across his brow.

"Very easy say Browndean. So easy!" cried Michael. "Easy say. Anything's easy say, when you can say it. What I don't like's total disappearance of an uncle. Not businesslike." And he nodded his head groggily.

"It's all perfectly simple," said Morris, desperately trying to pull himself together. "He's at Browndean recuperating from the railway crash."

"Aha, valuable uncle dead—an'—bury?" suggested Michael.

Morris sprang from his seat. "What's that you say?" he gasped.

"Oh! Now I've upset this bottle. Still exc'lent thing whiskey. Poor carpet. Give my love to Uncle Whiskey."

"You're not going away?" said Morris.

"Awf'ly sorry. Exc'lent whiskey," said the wavering Michael.

"I forbid you to go until you have explained your hints," growled Morris. "What do you mean? What brought you here?"

"No offense, I trust," mumbled Michael as he groped his way to the front door.

A carriage was waiting by the curb. The tired driver looked up as the lawyer approached, and asked where he was to go next.

Michael noticed that Morris had followed at his heels. A brilliant inspiration came to him. "Drive Shotland Yard," he ordered. "There's something devilish fishy, cabby, about those cousins. Mush be cleared up! Drive Shotland Yard!"

"You don't mean that, sir," said the driver

soothingly. "I had better take you home, sir. You can go to Scotland Yard tomorrow."

"All righ', never mind Shotland Yard. Drive Gaiety bar!" cried Michael.

"The Gaiety bar is closed," said the man.

"Then home," said Michael, with the same cheerfulness. "No. 23 King's Road. Drive there if you can see the way."

CHAPTER X

A Wild Chase

WITH BRIEFCASE IN HAND, Gideon felt himself a man at last. "Just last week," he mused, as the train sped across the English countryside, "I was a careless young dog with no thought but to be comfortable. I cared only for boating and detective novels. But now Miss Julia has changed all that! How a man ripens with the years."

Gideon had carried Julia straight to Uncle Hugh's house, and that gentleman, having been led to understand that she was the victim of oppression, noisily adopted her cause.

Julia must be kept out of the way, Uncle Hugh promptly decided. His houseboat was lying ready. There is no place like a houseboat for concealment. That very morning, in the teeth of an easterly gale, Uncle Hugh and Julia had embarked on their untimely voyage. Gideon pleaded in vain to be allowed to join the party. "No, Gid," said his uncle. "You are most certainly being watched. Keep away from us." Gideon gave in, for he feared if he rubbed off any of the romance that Uncle Hugh might grow weary of the whole affair.

Gideon was startled from his daydreams as, with a screeching of brakes, the train drew to a halt. But now it began to rain surprises. In all Hampton Court, there was no Shady Villa, no Selena Tarnow. This was strange, but perhaps his client had made some fatal oversight in the address. What was the next thoroughly prompt, manly, and businesslike step? thought Gideon. "A telegram," he answered himself at once. Seconds later, the wires were flashing the following message: "Dickson, The Royal Hotel. Villa and person both unknown here, suppose mistaken address. Arrive next train. Forsyth."

Within the hour Gideon charged into the lobby of The Royal Hotel. There are some days when it is better to have stayed in bed. No Selena Tarnow was one thing. No John Dickson and no Ezra Thomas, quite another. Questions danced in his bewildered brain. Pulling together the last shreds of his dignity, the tormented lawyer drove furiously for home. There was a cave of refuge, a place to think in. He climbed the stairs two at a time, put his key in the lock, and opened the door.

Night had fallen, and the apartment was pitch-black, but Gideon knew where the matches were kept and he strode purposefully across the room. A moment later, he collided with a heavy body, where no heavy body should have been. There had been nothing there when Gideon went out. He had locked the door behind him, he had found it locked upon his return. No one could have entered, the furniture could not have changed its own position. Yet, undeniably, there was something there. He thrust out his hands in the darkness. Yes, there was something, something large, something smooth, something cold.

"Oh!" cried Gideon, in surprise, "it feels like a piano."

He remembered leaving a book of matches in his pocket, and a moment later the pale light revealed the costly instrument, stained from rain water and defaced with recent scratches. In the far end of the room, the shadow of the strange visitor loomed bulkily and wavered on the wall.

With trembling hands, Gideon lit a lamp and drew near. Near or far, there was no doubt about it: the thing was a piano. There, where by all the laws of God and man it was impossible that it should be—there the thing stood. He threw open the keyboard and struck a chord. Not a sound disturbed the quiet of the room. "Is there something wrong with me?" he thought, with a pang. Again and again, he struck the soundless keys. Silence. Finally he gave the Broadwood two great bangs with his clenched fists. All was as still as the grave.

The young lawyer rose slowly to his feet.

"I am stark-raving mad," he cried aloud, "and no one knows it but myself. God's worst curse has fallen on me."

He snatched his watch from his pocket and held it to his ear. He could hear it ticking.

"I am not deaf," he said aloud. "I am only insane. My mind has quitted me forever."

He looked uneasily about the room, gazing with lackluster eyes at the chair where Mr. Dickson had sat. The end of a cigar lay near it in an ash tray.

"No," he thought, "I don't believe that was a dream, but God knows my mind is failing rapidly. I seem to be hungry, for instance. It's probably another hallucination. Still, I'll have one more good meal. I shall go to the corner cafe, and may possibly be carted from there direct to an asylum."

He wondered with morbid interest, as he walked along the street, how he would first betray his terrible condition. Would he attack a waiter? Or eat glass? He looked back at his house, with a lurking fear that there was no such place.

The brightly-lit entrance of the cafe calmed his fears. Besides, he was cheered to recognize his favorite waiter. His order appeared to be coherent. The dinner, when it came, was quite a tasty meal, and he ate it with enjoyment. "Upon my word," he mused, "I am about to indulge a hope. Have I been hasty?" Like all men in distress, Gideon decided to do what Napoleon, what Shakespeare, what Alexander the Great would have done. There remained only the minor question, What is that? The only thing that Gideon could think of to do was return to his apartment.

An hour later, he stood staring pitifully at the instrument of his confusion. To touch the keys was more than he dared venture. Whether they would remain silent, or suddenly resound with music, would be equally unnerving. "This may be a practical joke," he reflected, "though it seems elaborate and costly. Yet, what else could it be? It *must* be a practical joke." Just then his eye fell upon the key. "Why that?" he asked himself. "And why is it so conspicuously placed?" He circled around the piano, and sighted the keyhole at the back. "Aha! This is what the key is for. They wanted me to look inside. Stranger and stranger." Gingerly, he turned the key and raised the lid.

In what fits of agony, in what collapses of despair, Gideon passed the night.

That tiny trill of song with which the birds of London welcome the approach of day, found him limp and rumpled and bloodshot, and with a mind vacant of any inspiration. He rose and looked out upon the empty street and the gray daylight dotted with yellow lamps. There are mornings when the city seems to awake with a sick headache. This was one of them.

"Another day," Gideon thought, "and I am still helpless! This must come to an end." He locked up the piano, put the key in his pocket, and set forth in search of coffee. As he walked, his mind was fraught with a hundred terrors, misgivings, and regrets. He considered the obvious course of action: call in the police, give up the body, cover London with handbills describing his former clients. But no! The papers would be filled with the sordid affair. He would be the laughingstock of England. A child would have seen through the story of those adventurers, and he had gaped and swallowed it whole. Any self-respecting lawyer should have refused to listen to clients who came before him in such an irregular manner. And he had not only listened, he had gone upon an errand as well. What's more, he had taken their money! "No!" he wailed aloud. "I am dishonored! I have smashed my career for a five-pound note."

Between the possibility of being hanged in all innocence, and the certainty of a public disgrace, no man could long hesitate. After three gulps of hot, muddy coffee, Gideon's mind was made up. He would do without the police.

Now he must face the other side of the dilemma in earnest. How does a gentleman dispose of a dead body? It was impossible to prop a corpse on the corner of Tottenham Court Road without arousing fatal curiosity. As for lowering it down a London chimney, the physical obstacles were insurmountable. To get it on board a train and drop it out, or on the top of a bus and drop it off, were equally out of the question. To get it on a yacht and drop it overboard was more feasible, but for a man of limited means it seemed extravagant. The cost of renting a yacht was in itself a consideration, but the support of the necessary crew was simply not to be thought about.

All at once, an idea flashed through Gideon's murky mind. A houseboat was what he needed! A musical composer might very well suffer from the disturbances of London. He might very well be pressed for time to finish an opera. The whole character of the tormented musician and his music arose in bulk in Gideon's imagination. What would be more likely than a musician's arrival with his very own grand piano, and his residence in a houseboat, alone with an unfinished score? His final disappearance, leaving nothing behind but an empty piano case, might be more difficult to account for. And yet even that could be explained. For suppose the musician had gone mad over the finale, had destroyed his instrument in frustration, and then plunged into the cold river? What end would be more probable for a musical genius?

"By Jove, I'll do it!" cried Gideon.

CHAPTER XI

The Body
Goes to Sea?

෯෨෯෨෯෨෯෨෯෨෯෨෯෨෯෨෯

UNCLE HUGH HAVING ANNOUNCED his intention to
stay in Brighton, what would be more logical
than for Gideon to choose the quiet harbor of
Padwick? Near this pleasant riverside village he remembered having seen an ancient, weedy houseboat lying moored beside a tuft of willows. In his
careless hours, it had stirred in him a certain sense
of the romantic.

The total population of Padwick numbering in the vicinity of twenty, Gideon had little difficulty in finding the man in charge of the houseboat, and still less in persuading him to rent it. The fee was low, the acquisition immediate, the key was exchanged against a suitable advance in money, and Gideon returned to London by the afternoon train to arrange for his piano.

"I will be back tomorrow," he had said reassuringly. "I must get right to work on my opera."

And, sure enough, the next day Gideon found himself walking along the riverside road, carrying a basket of provisions in one hand, and a leather case in the other. It was October weather. The stone-gray sky was full of larks, bright autumnal foliage was reflected in the leaden mirror of the Thames, and fallen leaves littered the ground. There is no time of the year in England more invigorating, and Gideon, though he was not without his troubles, whistled as he went.

A little beyond Padwick, the river lies undisturbed. The region is uninhabited and few people penetrate the still waters. On the near side winds a path bordered by willows. There lay the houseboat, a thing so darkened by the overhanging willows, so grown upon by parasites, so decayed, so battered, so neglected, such a haunt of rats, that the heart of a new occupant might well recoil.

A plank, in the form of a drawbridge, joined it to the shore. It was a dreary moment for Gideon when he pulled the plank in after him and found himself alone on this unwholesome fortress. He could hear the rats scuttle and flop in the abhorred interior. The cabin was deep in dust, and smelled strongly of stagnant water. It could not be called a cheerful spot, even for a composer absorbed in beloved toil. How much less cheerful it was for a young man haunted by fears and awaiting the arrival of a corpse.

Gideon sat down, cleared away a corner of the table, and attacked the cold luncheon in his basket. In the case of any later investigation, it was desirable that he should be seen as little as possible. If he could stand it, the day should be spent entirely inside the cabin. In keeping with his scheme, he had brought along a ream of large-size music paper.

"Now to work," he said, when he had satisfied his appetite. "I must leave traces of the wretched man's activity." And he began to scrawl musical notes across the paper.

Soon the penetrating chill of the river began to seep up through the floor of the cabin. To the audible annoyance of the rats, Gideon began walking briskly from one end of the room to the other. He was still cold. "This is all nonsense," he whined.

"I don't care about the risk, but I refuse to catch pneumonia. I must get out in the sunlight."

He stepped out on deck, looking up the river for the first time. He started. Only a few hundred yards away, another houseboat lay moored among the willows. It was very spick-and-span, an elegant canoe hung at the stern, the windows were concealed by snowy curtains, a flag waved from the bow. The more Gideon looked at it, the more it looked like his uncle's houseboat. It was exceedingly like it, almost identical. But for the fact that Gideon knew his uncle was at Brighton, he could have sworn it was the same. Yet, it did bear a very strong resemblance.

As Gideon continued studying the houseboat, the door suddenly opened and a young woman stepped out on deck. There was no mistaking Miss Julia! Gideon fled into his cabin. Through the window, he watched her draw in the canoe, get on board, cast off, and come sailing downstream in his direction.

"Well, everything's over now," he wailed, clutching at the wall of the cabin.

"Good afternoon, Miss," said a voice on the water. Gideon recognized the nasal tones of his landlord.

"Good afternoon," replied Julia, "but I don't know who you are, do I? Oh, yes, I do though. You are the nice man who gave me permission to sketch this old houseboat."

Gideon's heart leaped with fear.

"That's right," said the man. "I'm sorry, but you can't do it any more. You see, I've rented it."

"Rented it!" cried Julia.

"Rented it for a month," said the man. "Seems strange, don't it? Can't see what the party wants with it!"

"It seems very romantic of him, I think," said Julia. "What sort of person is he?"

Julia in her canoe, the landlord in his rowboat, were close alongside, and holding on to the stern of the houseboat, so that not a word was lost on Gideon.

"He's a music man," said the landlord, "or at least that's what he told me, Miss. He come down here to write an op'ra."

"Really!" cried Julia. "I've never heard of anything so delightful! Why, we shall be able to slip down at night and hear him improvise! Whatever can his opera be about?" And Gideon heard her laughter ripple across the water. "We must try to get acquainted with this composer. I feel sure he must be very nice."

"Well, Miss, I'm afraid I must be moving along."

"Oh, don't let me keep you, you kind man!" said Julia. "Good afternoon."

"Good afternoon to you, Miss."

Gideon sat in the cabin, a prey to the most harrowing thoughts. Here he was anchored to a rotting houseboat, soon to be anchored to it still more by the corpse. All around him, the country was buzzing with young ladies proposing pleasure parties to surround his house at night. Well, that meant the gallows. But what was worse, if anything could be, was Miss Julia's tendency to strike up an acquaintance with anybody. She had no reserve. She was on a familiar footing with a brute like his landlord. She took an immediate and obvious interest in the yet-to-appear composer. He could imagine her asking the composer to have tea with her! And it was to a girl like this that Gideon had offered his heart!

Gideon's thoughts were interrupted by a sound that sent him whipping behind the door. Miss Julia had stepped on board the houseboat. Judging from her manner, she obviously supposed that the composer had not as yet arrived, and she had decided to take advantage of this fact and complete her sketch. Down she sat in the bow, produced her artist's pad and watercolors, and was soon busily at work.

Meanwhile, Gideon stood behind the door, afraid to move, afraid to breathe, afraid to think, confined by fatigue and tedium. This could not, he reflected with gratitude, last forever. Even the gallows could not fail to be a relief.

Just then, around a bend in the river, a steamboat made an untimely entrance. All along the banks the water swelled and fell, and the reeds rustled. The houseboat itself became suddenly imbued with life, and rolled briskly at her moorings, like a seagoing ship when she begins to smell the open ocean.

The waves had nearly died away, and the quick panting of the steamboat already sounded faint and far off, when Gideon was startled by a cry from Julia. Peering through the window, he beheld her staring woefully downstream at the fast-vanishing canoe. Gideon foresaw in an instant what was about to follow. With one quick movement of his body, he dropped to the floor and crawled under the table.

Julia, on her part, was not yet totally aware of her plight. She saw that she had lost the canoe and she looked forward with little enthusiasm to her next meeting with Uncle Hugh, but she had no idea that she was imprisoned, for she knew about the drawbridge.

She made the tour of the houseboat and found the door open and the bridge withdrawn. It was plain, then, that the composer must have already arrived. Plain, too, that he must be on board. He must be a very shy man to have put up with this invasion of his residence and made no sign. Julia's courage rose higher at the thought. She must force him from his privacy, for the plank was too heavy for her to lift alone. She tapped upon the open door. Then she tapped again.

"Oh!" she cried. "Please come out! You must come, you know, sooner or later, for I can't manage this plank without you. Oh, please, come!"

Still there was no reply.

"If he *is* here he must be angry," she thought fearfully. But the next moment, she imagined that he might have gone on an excursion. In that case, she could explore the houseboat. She pushed upon the door and stepped down into the cabin. Under the table, where he lay smothered with dust, Gideon's heart stood still.

Julia sighted the remains of Gideon's lunch. "He rather likes nice things to eat," she thought. "Oh, I am quite sure that he is a delightful man. I wonder if he is as good-looking as Gideon Forsyth. And here is some of his music, too. '*Adagio molto expressivo, sempre legato,*'" she read. "How very strange to have all these directions, and only three or four notes. Oh, dear me," she thought, glancing over the music, "he must be terribly modern in his approach. Let's try the melody. Somehow, it seems familiar." She began to sing it, and suddenly broke off with laughter. "Why, it's the national anthem!" She cried aloud. "The man must be a mere imposter."

Just at this moment there came a confused, scuffling sound from underneath the table. A strange gasp ushered in an explosive sneeze. The head of the sufferer was at the same time brought in contact with the boards above, and the sneeze was followed by a hollow groan.

Julia fled for the door, then turned and bravely faced the danger. There was no pursuit. The sounds continued. Below the table, a crouching figure was contending with a sneezing fit. That was all.

"Surely," thought Julia, "this is most unusual behavior. What sort of man can this composer be?"

Meanwhile, the dust of years had been disturbed by Gideon's convulsions, and the sneezing fit was followed by a spasm of coughing.

Julia began to feel a certain interest. "I am afraid you are really quite ill," she said, drawing a little nearer. "Please don't let me disturb you, and please do not stay under that table. Indeed, it cannot be good for you."

A distressing cough was the reply, and the next moment Julia was on her knees, and their faces had almost knocked together under the table.

"Oh, my gracious goodness!" Julia exclaimed, springing to her feet. "Gideon gone mad!"

"I am not mad," said Gideon ruefully, extricating himself from his position. "Dearest Julia, I swear to you upon my knees I am not mad!"

"Oh, poor insane Gideon!" she cried.

"I know," he said, "that to the naked eye my conduct may appear unconventional."

"If you are not mad, that was no way to behave," cried Julia. "You must not care one penny for my feelings!"

"That's hardly the case!" objected Gideon violently.

"It was abominable conduct!" exclaimed Julia.

"I know that it must have lowered your opinion of me," said Gideon sadly, "but, dearest Julia, I beg of you, let me explain. I positively cannot and will not agree to continue living without the esteem of one whom I admire. The moment is ill-chosen, I am well aware of that, but I repeat the expression—one whom I admire."

"Very well," she said, "come out of this dreadfully cold place, and let's sit down on deck." Gideon dutifully followed her. "Now," she began, making herself comfortable against the railing of the houseboat, "start explaining. I'll hear you out." And then, seeing him stand before her so uncomfortably, she was suddenly overcome with laughter.

Julia's laugh was a thing to melt icebergs. There was but one creature who heard it without joy, and that was her unfortunate admirer.

"Miss Julia," he said, in a voice edged with annoyance, "I beg of you, do not treat me and my plight so lightly."

Julia made great eyes at him.

"Already the freedom with which I heard you hobnobbing with my landlord gave me exquisite pain. Then there was your lack of feminine reserve about the composer . . ."

"But that composer appears to be yourself," objected Julia.

"I am far from denying that," cried Gideon, "but you did not know it at the time. It cut me to the heart."

"Really, this all seems very silly," replied Julia. "You have behaved in the most extraordinary manner, you pretend to explain your conduct, and instead of doing just that, you begin to attack me."

"You must forgive me. Perhaps I *was* too hasty," said Gideon. "I—I will make a clean breast of it. When you know all the circumstances you might be able to excuse me."

And sitting down beside her on the deck, he recounted his miserable tale.

"Oh, Gideon," she cried, when he had finished, "I am so sorry! I wish I hadn't laughed at you, only you were so exceedingly funny. But I wish I hadn't, and I wouldn't have either if I had only known." And she gave him her hand.

Gideon enclosed it with his own. "You do not think the worse of me for this?" he asked tenderly.

"Because you have been so silly and gotten into such a dreadful dilemma? You poor boy, no!" cried Julia, and in the warmth of the moment, pressed her other hand into his. "You may count on me," she added.

"Really?" asked Gideon.

"Really and really!" replied Julia.

"I do then, and I will," cried Gideon emotionally. "I admit that the moment is not well chosen, but I have no friends to speak of."

"Nor do I," said Julia. "But don't you think it's perhaps about time you gave me back my hands?"

"Please, the merest moment more!" cried Gideon. "I have so few friends," he added.

"I thought it was considered a bad sign for a young man to have no friends," observed Julia.

"Oh, but I have crowds of *friends!*" cried Gideon. "That's not what I mean. I feel the moment is ill-chosen, but oh, Miss Julia, if you could only see yourself!"

"Please," said Julia, "we have know each other such a short time."

"Not at all!" protested Gideon. "We met at Morris Finsbury's house ever so long ago. I never forgot you since. Say you never forgot me!"

"Isn't this rather—sudden?" asked Julia.

"Oh, you may laugh at me to your heart's delight!" cried Gideon. "Oh, yes, I mean to win you, Miss Julia. I am in dreadful trouble, and I have not a penny of my own, and yet I mean to win you. Look at me, if you can, and tell me no!"

She looked at him, and whatever her eyes may have told him, it is to be supposed he took pleasure in the message, for he read it a long while.

"And Uncle Hugh will give us some money to live on in the meantime," he said, at last.

"Well, I call that cool!" said a cheerful voice at his elbow.

Gideon and Julia sprang apart. Uncle Hugh, coming up the river in his boat, had captured the truant canoe, and guessing what had happened, had planned to surprise Julia at her sketching. He had unexpectedly brought down two birds with one stone. As he looked upon the pair of flushed and breathless culprits, the human instinct of the matchmaker softened his heart.

"Well, I call that cool," he repeated, "you seem to count very securely upon Uncle Hugh. But look here, Gideon, I thought I had told you to keep away?"

"To keep away from Brighton," replied Gideon. "How did I know you'd be *here?*"

"Well, you have a point there," admitted Uncle Hugh. "You see I thought it would be better if even you did not know of my address. Those rascals, Morris and John Finsbury, would have wormed it out of you. But listen, Gideon, you promised me you would get to work, and here I find you playing the fool at Padwick."

"Please, you must not be cross with poor Gideon," pleaded Julia. "He is in dreadful trouble."

"What's this all about, Gideon?" asked his uncle. "Have you been fighting? Do you owe someone money?"

"It's much worse than that," said Gideon. "A syndicate of murderers seems to have deposited a corpse in my midst. It's legal business after all, you see!" And with these words, Gideon, for the second time that day, began to describe the adventure with the piano.

"I must write to *The Times,*" cried Uncle Hugh.

"Do you want to get me disbarred?" asked Gideon.

"Disbarred! Come, it can't be as bad as that."

"It wouldn't do, Uncle Hugh," said Gideon.

"But you're not crazy enough," cried his uncle, "to continue trying to dispose of the body yourself?"

"There is no other path open to me," said Gideon.

"It's not common sense, and I will not hear of it," cried Uncle Hugh. "I command you, Gideon, to desist from this criminal interference."

"Very well, then, I hand it over to you," said Gideon, "and you can do what you like with the dead body."

"Not on your life!" exclaimed the uncle. "I'll have nothing to do with it."

"Then you must allow me to do the best I can," retorted his nephew. "Believe me, I have a distinct talent for this sort of difficulty."

"As you wish. *I* will have no hand in the thing. Come to think of it, it's highly undesirable that either I or Miss Julia should linger here. We might be observed," said Uncle Hugh, looking up and down the river. "And, at any rate, it's time for dinner."

"What?" cried Gideon, plunging for his watch. "And so it is! Great guns, the piano should have been here hours ago!"

Uncle Hugh was clambering back into his boat, but at these words he paused.

"I saw it arrive myself at the station, and hired a mover. He had a delivery to make, but he was to be here by four at the latest," cried Gideon, now on the borderline of hysteria. "No doubt the piano is open, and the body found."

"You must flee at once," cried Uncle Hugh. "It's the only manly step."

"But suppose everything's all right?" wailed Gideon. "Suppose the piano comes, and I am not not here to receive it? I will have hanged myself by my cowardice. No, Uncle Hugh, inquiries must be made at the railroad station. I dare not go, of course, but you may. You could hang around the police office, don't you see?"

"No, Gideon, my dear nephew. I regard you with the most sacred affection. But no—not the police."

"Then you desert me?" said Gideon. "Say it plainly."

"Far from it! Far from it!" protested Uncle Hugh. "I only propose caution. Common sense, Gideon, should always be an Englishman's guide."

"Will you both let me speak?" said Julia. "I think that Gideon had better leave this dreadful houseboat, and wait among the willows over there. If the piano comes, then he could step out and claim it. If the police come, he could slip into our houseboat until the coast is clear."

"This young lady has strong common sense," said Uncle Hugh.

"Oh, I don't think I'm at all a fool," said Julia, with conviction.

"But what if neither of them come?" asked Gideon. "What should I do then?"

"Why then," replied Julia, "you had better go down to the village after dark and investigate. I can go with you, and then I am sure that you would never be suspected. Even if you were, I could tell them it was a mistake."

"I will not allow Miss Julia to go," cried Uncle Hugh.

"Why?" asked Julia.

Uncle Hugh had not the slightest desire to tell her why, for it was simply his own fear of being drawn into the sordid business himself. But with the usual tactics of a man who is ashamed of himself, he took the high hand. "My dear Miss Julia, your reputation . . . " he began weakly.

"Oh, is that all?" interrupted Julia. "Then the three of us must go."

"Caught!" thought the uncle.

CHAPTER XII

Swan Song

A REALLY NOTEWORTHY THING was taking place not far from Padwick. On the bench of a delivery cart there sat a tow-headed, lanky youth. The reins were on his lap, the whip lay behind him in the interior of the cart, and the horse trotted along at a leisurely pace without guidance or encouragement. The driver, his gaze dwelling on the skies, devoted himself entirely to a brand-new penny whistle.

The tow-headed youth had just begun that pleasing melody "The Ploughboy" for the nineteeth time, when he was struck into extreme confusion by the discovery that he was not alone.

"There! You have it now!" cried a hearty voice from the side of the road. "That's as good as I want to hear!"

The boy glanced, from the depths of his humiliation, at the speaker. He beheld a powerful, tanned, clean-shaven fellow, about forty years old, striding beside the cart. The man's clothes were shabby, but he looked proud and self-reliant.

"I'm only a beginner," gasped the blushing youth, "I didn't think anybody could hear me."

"Well, I like that!" the man exclaimed. "You're a pretty old beginner. Come, let me have a seat beside you, and I'll sing along." The next moment, the man was perched on the cart. "I even play a little myself," he added, reaching for the whistle. He gave the instrument a knowing look, mouthed it, and dashed into "The Girl I left Behind Me." He was a great performer. As the boy listened, jealousy gave way to generous enthusiasm.

"Your turn," said the man, offering the whistle.

"Oh, not after you!" cried the youth. "You're a professional."

"No," said his companion, "an amateur like yourself. I have my style of playing, you have yours.

Yours, of course, is better. But I began when I was a boy, you see, before my taste was formed. When you're my age, you'll probably play before the queen. Play that melody you were playing before. How does it go again?"

A timid, insane hope sprang in the breast of the boy. Was it possible? Was there something in his playing, after all? It had, indeed, seemed to him at times as if he got a kind of richness out of it. Was he a genius? Meanwhile, his traveling companion stumbled over the melody.

"No," said the youth, "That's not quite it. It goes this way. Here, I'll show you."

And, taking the whistle between his lips, he sealed his doom. When he had played the tune through, and then repeated it a second time, and then a third; when his companion had tried it once more, and once more failed; when it became clear to the boy that he, the blushing amateur, was actually giving a lesson to this full-grown flutist, floods of glory seemed to brighten the autumnal countryside. As the youth played on and on, the older man listened and approved.

As he listened, however, he took care to look both before and behind the cart. He looked behind and computed the value of the delivery boy's load, noting the paper-wrapped parcels, and briefly remarking the grand piano as "difficult to get rid of." Then, he looked ahead of him, spying at the corner of a green lane a little public inn.

"Come, my lad, I'll treat you to a friendly glass," the man invited winningly.

In the Blue Lion, the older man introduced his willing friend to a number of ingenious mixtures. The most effective of these was a pint of mild ale laced with twopence worth of London gin. Its effect upon the youth was revolutionary. He had to be helped on board his own cart, hooting with laughter and riotous song.

His companion, meanwhile, quietly helped himself to the reins. It was plain he had a taste for the more secluded beauties of the English landscape, for the cart, under his guidance, never chose the dusty highway, preferring to journey between hedge and ditch, and for the most part, under overhanging boughs. It was plain, too, that he had an eye to the true interests of the young delivery boy, for the cart drew up more than once at the doors of public inns along the rural drive.

A little after nightfall, the cart was brought to a standstill in a woody road. The older man lifted the inanimate form of the boy from among the parcels, and tenderly deposited it upon the wayside.

"If you come to before daylight," thought the thief, "I, for one, shall be surprised."

From the pockets of the slumbering delivery boy,

he gently collected the sum of seventeen shillings. Then, getting into the cart once more, he drove thoughtfully away.

"If I only knew where I was, it would be a good job," he mused. "Anyway, here's a corner."

He turned it, and found himself upon the riverside. A little beyond him, the lights of a houseboat shone cheerfully. And already close at hand, so close that it was impossible to avoid them, three persons, a lady and two gentlemen, were deliberately drawing near. The thief put his trust in the convenient darkness of the night, and drove on to meet them. One of the gentlemen walked to the middle of the road and held up a cane by way of signal.

"My man, have you seen anything of a delivery cart?" he cried.

Dark as it was, it seemed to the thief as though the younger of the two gentlemen had made a motion to prevent the other from speaking. At another time, the thief would have paid more attention to the fact, but he was then too immersed in the perils of his own predicament.

"A delivery cart?" he asked, uneasily. "No, sir, I don't think I have."

"Ah!" said the older gentleman, and stood aside to let the cart pass, but the lady appeared to bend forward and study the cart with sharpened curiosity.

"I wonder what the devil they're up to," thought the thief. Looking back fearfully, he saw the trio standing together in the middle of the road, like folk consulting. The word "detective" flashed through his mind and, vigorously applying the whip, he fled up the riverside road in terror. The lights of the houseboat streaked by the flying cart. Soon, the beat of hoofs and the rattle of the cart died away and, to the trio on the road, silence fell.

"It's the most extraordinary thing," cried Gideon, "but that's the cart!"

"And I know I saw a piano," added Julia.

"Oh, it's the cart, certainly," said Gideon, "but the extraordinary thing is, it's not the man."

"It must be the man, Gideon, it must be!" exclaimed Uncle Hugh.

"Well, then, why is he running away?" asked Gideon.

"His horse bolted, I suppose," replied the uncle.

"Nonsense! I heard the whip going like a flail," said Gideon. "It simply defies human reason."

"I'll tell you," interrupted Julia, "he came around that corner. Suppose we went and followed his trail? There may be a house there, or somebody who saw him, or something."

"Well, suppose we did, just for the fun of it," said Gideon.

The fun of it, more properly defined, consisted of passing time with Julia. To Uncle Hugh, who was excluded from these simple pleasures, the excursion appeared hopeless from the start. So, when a fresh perspective of darkness opened up, dimly contained between the black outlines of the forest on the one side and a hedge and ditch upon the other, the portly uncle drew to a halt.

"This is a wild-goose chase," he said firmly.

A moment later, a low moan shattered the silence.

"Oh, what's that?" cried Julia.

"I can't think," said Gideon, walking in the direction of the moan.

"Oh, Gideon!" wailed Julia. "Stay away from it! It might be something perfectly horrid!"

"It may be the devil himself," said Gideon, "but I'm going to see it."

"Don't be rash," pleaded his uncle.

As Gideon drew nearer to the sound, a dark object, not unlike a human form, appeared on the brink of the ditch.

"It's a man," said Gideon, "it's only a man. He appears to be asleep and snoring, but there must be something wrong with him, he won't awaken."

Gideon struck a match, and by its light recognized the tow-head of the delivery boy.

"Here he is, the one I hired!" cried Gideon. "But he's as drunk as this forest is dark! I see the whole story now." His two companions, who had now ventured to rejoin him, listened as he offered an explanation for the strange state of things.

"Drunken brute!" exclaimed Uncle Hugh. "Let's give him what he deserves!"

"Not at all," said Gideon. "It is highly undesirable that he should see us together. Do you know, my uncle, that I am very much obliged to him, for this is about the luckiest thing that could have possibly happened. It seems to be that I'm clear of it at last!"

"Clear of what?" asked Uncle Hugh.

"The whole affair!" cried Gideon. "That man we saw earlier has been stupid enough to steal the cart and the dead body. What he hopes to do with it, I neither know nor care. My hands are free! Julia, my darling girl, Julia, I. . ."

"Gideon! Gideon," said his uncle.

"Oh, it's all right when we're going to be married so soon," said Gideon. "You know, you said so yourself in the houseboat."

"I did?" said Uncle Hugh. "I am certain I said no such thing."

"Appeal to him, tell him he did, get on his soft side!" cried Gideon.

"I know Gideon will be so good," said Julia, turning to Uncle Hugh. "He has promised to apply himself to his law career, and I will see that he does it too. And you know that marriage is very steadying to young men, though, of course, I have no money," she added.

"My dear young lady, as my nephew told you today, Uncle Hugh has plenty, and I can never forget how that vile Morris Finsbury treated you. But now, let us get back to the houseboat. We return to London at once."

"Yes!" cried Gideon. "Tomorrow there will be no houseboat, and no composer, and no delivery cart, and no piano. And when this boy awakes, he may tell himself the whole affair has been a dream."

"Aha!" said Uncle Hugh, "but there's another man who will have a different awakening. That fellow in the cart will find he has been too clever."

"Uncle Hugh and Julia," said Gideon, "I am finished with all my troubles, Julia's hand is in mine. Is this a time for anything but loving sentiments? When I think of that poor unhappy devil in the cart, I stand here in the night and cry for him with all my heart."

"Amen," said Uncle Hugh.

CHAPTER XIII

The Tribulations
of Morris

THE MORNING AFTER HIS SESSION with Michael, Morris rose from the leaden slumber of distress to find his hand tremulous, his throat parched, and his digestion obviously paralyzed. "Lord knows it's not from eating!" Morris thought, and as he dressed he reviewed his various anxieties.

Anxiety the First: *Where Is the Body?* It was now plain that William Dent Pitman belonged to the darker order of the criminal class. An honest man would not have cashed the check. A humane man would not have accepted in silence the tragic contents of the barrel. A man, who was not already up to the chin in gore, would have lacked the means for secretly disposing of the body. This process of reasoning left a horrid image of the monster, Pitman. Doubtless, he had disposed of the body long ago, dropping it through a trapdoor in his kitchen, Morris supposed. The man most probably now lived in wanton splendor on the proceeds from the check. So far, all was peace. But with the habits of a man like Pitman, eight hundred pounds could be easily melted in a week. When they were spent, what could he be likely to do next? A voice in Morris' own bosom gave the answer: "Blackmail me."

Anxiety the Second: *The Tontine or Is My Uncle Masterson Dead?* This question, on which all Morris' hopes depended, was yet to be answered. He had tried to bully Michael's housekeeper, Teena. He had tried to bribe her and nothing came of it. He had considered blackmailing Michael, but even less came of that. Besides, was Michael the man to be blackmailed? And was Morris the man to do it? Grave considerations. "It's not that I'm afraid of him," Morris reassured himself, "it's just that I must be very sure of my ground."

Anxiety the Third: *The Underpaid Accomplice.* For he had an accomplice, and that accomplice was rotting away in a damp cottage somewhere in England with empty pockets. What could be done about that? He really should have sent John something. "But how?" Morris asked himself, ruefully pouring into his hand a half-crown, a florin, and eightpence in small change. For a man in Morris' position, at war with all society, and conducting, with the hand of inexperience, a vast intrigue, the sum was really laughable. John would have to make the best of it. "But then," asked the voice, "how long is John likely to stand it?"

Anxiety the Fourth: *The Leather Business*. Morris had not yet dared to visit the family firm. Yet, he knew he must delay no longer. Well and good, but what was he to do there? He had no right to sign checks in his own name, and he seemed to lack the art of signing with his uncle's. Under these circumstances, he could do nothing to procrastinate the crash. When it came, two questions could not fail to be addressed to a speechless and perspiring Morris. Where is Mr. Joseph Finsbury? How about your visit to the bank? Questions like that could so easily lead to the gallows.

Morris was trying to shave when an idea struck him, and he laid the razor down. There was, in Michael's words, the total disappearance of a valuable uncle. There was a time of mysterious conduct on the part of a nephew who had been in bad blood with the old man through seven years. "But no," thought Morris, "they cannot dare to think I'd murder him. Not that. But honestly, speaking man to man, I don't see any other crime that I don't seem somehow to have committed. And yet, I'm a perfectly respectable man."

With this conclusion firmly seated in his mind, Morris Finsbury, still half-shaven, went to collect the morning mail. There was a letter in the box. He knew the handwriting. John at last!

"Well, I think I might have been spared this," he said bitterly, tearing the envelope open.

"Dear Morris," he read aloud, "whatever is going on? I'm in an awful hole down here. I can't stand it, nobody could. I would have left here before, only I have no money for the train. Don't be a lunatic, Morris. You don't seem to understand my dreadful situation. Ever your affectionate brother, John Finsbury."

"Oh, what can I do for him?" Morris asked himself. Cramming the letter in his pocket, he left the house. "How can I send anybody money? At least, he can't cut and run. He's got to stay. He's as helpless as the dead. Complains, does he? Why, he's never even heard of William Dent Pitman. If he had what I have on my mind, he'd have a right to complain."

But Morris could not forget that John was miserably trapped in that rotting house, without news, without money, without friends, or any entertainment. By the time he had been shaved and gulped down a hasty breakfast at the corner tavern, Morris had arrived at a compromise.

"Poor John," he said to himself, "he's in a frightful spot. I can't send him any money, but I'll send him *Naughty London by Night.* It'll cheer him up."

On his way to the leather business, Morris purchased a single copy of that enlivening periodical. So there was John set up with literature, and Morris' conscience was at peace.

As if to reward him, he was received in his place of business with good news. Orders were pouring in. Even the manager appeared elated. As for Morris, who had almost forgotten the meaning of good news, he longed to sob like a little child. He could have caught the manager to his bosom. He could have bestowed a check—for a small sum—to every clerk in the firm. As he sat and opened his letters, a joyous refrain rang through his thoughts, "This old business may be profitable yet, profitable yet, profitable yet."

But his sunny moment of relief was short-lived. The return of misfortune was signaled in the form of a creditor. Yet the appearance of Mr. Rodgers was surprising, for his connection with the firm was old and regular.

"Oh, Finsbury," Rodgers began uneasily, "it's only fair to let you know that money is a trifle tight. You see, my debts . . . everyone's complaining . . . and in short. . ."

"It has never been our habit, Rodgers," said Morris, turning pale, "but I'll see what I can do. I dare say we can let you have something on account."

"Well, quite frankly," Rodgers replied, with some embarrassment, "I've let the credit out of my hands."

"Out of your hands?" repeated Morris. "That's playing rather fast and loose with us, Rodgers."

"Sorry, Finsbury, but I couldn't wait any longer. Got the full amount, on the nail, in a certified check."

"The full amount!" cried Morris. "Who's the party?"

"Don't really know the man," was the reply. "Name of Elgin."

What could this Elgin want with a claim against the house of Finsbury? Morris asked himself, when his visitor was gone. And why should he pay the full amount for the credit? It proved his eagerness. The claim must have been wanted instantly, for that day, for that morning even. Why? "And just when all was looking well, too!" cried Morris.

A moment later, Mr. Elgin was announced. He was acting, it appeared, for a third party. He understood nothing of the circumstances. His client simply wanted the credit paid in full. Mr. Finsbury could date the check two months in advance, if he chose.

"What does this all mean?" asked Morris, in frustration. "What made you buy the credit from Rodgers?"

Mr. Elgin had no idea. He was only following orders.

"The whole affair is thoroughly irregular," said Morris angrily. "It is not the custom of the trade to settle debts at this time of year. What are your instructions if I refuse?"

"I am to see Mr. Joseph Finsbury, the head of the firm," replied Elgin. "My orders were to insist on that. It was implied, by my client, you had no status here."

"You can't see my Uncle Joseph. He's ill," said Morris.

"In that case, I was to place the matter in the hands of a lawyer," retorted Elgin. "Yes, a Mr. Michael Finsbury. A relative, perhaps? In that case, I presume, the matter will be pleasantly arranged."

To pass into Michael's hands was too much for Morris. A check dated two months in advance was nothing, after all. In two months he would probably be dead, or in jail at any rate. "I'm going over to get the check signed by Uncle Joseph," Morris said. "He is ill and can't leave the house."

A cab there and a cab back. He counted the cost. When he was done he would be left with three shillings to his name. What was even worse, he had been forced to pretend that Joseph was now in London. "What's the use of John staying on in Browndean," he reflected.

For once, Morris surprised himself. The forgery was a success, and within three quarters of an hour he handed it to Mr. Elgin.

"This is very satisfactory," observed Elgin, rising from his chair. "I was to tell you it will not be cashed, but you had better take care."

The room swam around Morris. "What's that!" he cried, grasping the table. He was miserably conscious the next moment of his shrill tongue and ashen face. "What do you mean, it will not be cashed? Why am I to take care? What's this all about?"

"I have no idea," replied Elgin, smiling.

"What is your client's name?" asked Morris.

"That is a secret for the moment," answered Elgin.

Morris bent toward him. "It's not the bank?" he asked hoarsely.

"I have no authority to say more," replied Elgin. "Now, I must wish you a good morning."

"Wish me a good morning!" thought Morris. A moment later, seizing his hat, he fled from his place of business like a madman. Three streets away, he stopped and groaned. "I should have borrowed from the manager!" he cried. "But it's too late now. I'm penniless like the unemployed."

He went home and sat in the dusty kitchen with his head in his hands. "The bad luck I've had is enough to breed a revolution," he moaned. "And the plain English of the thing is that I must have money at once. I'm done with all morality now. I'm long past due that stage. I must have money *now* and the only chance I see is William Dent Pitman. Pitman is a criminal, and therefore his position is weak. He must have some of that eight hundred pounds left. If he has, I'll force him to split it with me. And even if he hasn't, I'll tell him about the tontine affair."

Well and good. But how to contact Pitman, except by advertisement, was not so clear. And even so, on what grounds could he arrange a meeting? And where? Not at John Street, for it would never do to let a man like Pitman know your real address. And not at Pitman's house, probably some dreadful hideaway with a trapdoor in the kitchen. "I never dreamed that I would ever frequent such a society," Morris thought, with a shudder. Then an idea struck him. Waterloo Station, a public place, yet deserted during certain hours. Morris took a piece of paper and wrote his advertisement.

William Dent Pitman, be at Waterloo Station platform next Sunday from 2-4 p.m. *It is to your advantage.*

"Good," said Morris aloud. "That should smoke the criminal out!" And clutching the paper in his hand, he dashed out into the crowded street.

CHAPTER XIV
More Tribulations

SUNDAY MORNING, William Dent Pitman rose at his usual hour, although with something more than his usual reluctance. The day before, an addition had been made to his household in the person of a lodger. Michael Finsbury had acted as sponsor in the business and had guaranteed to foot the weekly bill. At first meeting, the talkative old gentleman appeared to be a lively acquisition, but as the day wore on Pitman had begun to entertain ideas of flight. Never in his life had he met such a boring man as Joseph Finsbury.

Still numb from the night before, Pitman entered the little kitchen, where the table was already laid for breakfast. "I trust you have slept well," he muttered, peering glassily at his new lodger.

"Accustomed as I have been to a life of almost perpetual change," replied Joseph, "the disturbance to one's habits so often complained of by the more sedentary, is something from which I am entirely free."

"I'm delighted to hear it," said Pitman thickly. "But I see I have interrupted your reading."

"The Sunday paper is one of the features of the age," began Joseph. "In America, I am told, it supersedes all other literature. Journalism caters to the masses. Hundreds of columns are occupied with interesting details of the world's doings, such as elopements, robberies, matricides, and public entertainment. There is a corner for politics, chess, religion, and even literature. A few spicy editorials serve to direct the course of public thought. It is difficult to estimate the part played by such enormous repositories in the education of the people. But although all this is interesting, I fear that I disgress. Are you yourself a student of the daily press?"

"There is not much in the papers to interest an artist," replied Pitman.

"In that case," continued Joseph, "an advertisement which has appeared the last two days in various papers, and reappears this morning, may possibly have failed to catch your eye. The name bears a strong resemblance to your own. Ah, there it is. If you please, I will read it to you.

" 'William Dent Pitman, be at Waterloo Station on the far end of the main departure platform from 2-4 p.m. today. *It is to your advantage.*' "

"Is that in print?" cried Pitman. "Let me see it! *'It is to my advantage'*? Mr. Finsbury, I am aware how strange this must sound to your ears, but there are domestic reasons why this little circumstance might perhaps be better kept between ourselves. Let me assure you that there is nothing dishonest in my secrecy. I may set your conscience at rest when I assure you all the circumstances are known to our common friend, your excellent nephew, Michael Finsbury."

"Say no more," said Joseph, with a sweep of his hand.

An hour later, Pitman found Michael in bed and reading a book, the very picture of good humor.

"Hello, Pitman," he said, laying down his book. "What brings you here at this unreasonable hour?"

"I am on the brink of something new," he said, presenting the advertisement to Michael.

"Why, what is this?" cried Michael, sitting up suddenly.

"It will have to be attended to," said Pitman.

"I thought you'd had enough of Waterloo Station," retorted Michael. "Have you developed a morbid craving?"

"Michael," said the artist, "I have tried to reason the matter out, and with your permission, I should like to lay the results before you."

"Fire away," said Michael, "but, please, Pitman, remember it's Sunday, and let's have no bad language."

"There are two possibilities," began Pitman. "First, this may be connected with the barrel. Second, it may be connected with Mr. Semitopolis' statue. In the second case, it is plainly my duty to leave no stone unturned for the recovery of the lost antique. I must behave like a gentleman."

"I have sometimes thought I should try and behave like a gentleman myself," said Michael, "only it's such a one-sided business, with the world and the legal profession being the way they are. To proceed, we have your second idea, that this has some connection with the statue. Possible. But in that case who is the advertiser? Not your Italian associate, for he knows your address. Not the person who got the packing case, for he doesn't know your name.

Possibly the moving man. He might have got your name, but he might have failed to get your address. Yes, perhaps it's the moving man. But do you really wish to meet the moving man?"

"Why not?" asked Pitman. "My duty to Mr. Semitopolis has no limits. I am going to Waterloo Station," he added, "in disguise."

"All by your little self?" asked Michael. "Well, I hope you think it safe. Don't forget to write me from the police cells."

"Oh, Michael, I had ventured to hope that perhaps you might be induced to come along," faltered Pitman.

"Disguise myself on Sunday?" cried Michael. "How little you understand my principles!"

"I have no means of showing you my gratitude, but let me ask you one question," said Pitman. "If I were a very rich client, would you not take the risk?"

"Why, my good fellow, do you think I make it a practice of trotting about London in disguise with my clients?" cried Michael. "Do you suppose money would induce me to touch this business with a ten-foot pole? I give you my word of honor, it would not. But I admit I have a real curiosity to see how you conduct this interview. That tempts me, Pitman, more than gold." And suddenly Michael laughed. "Well, Pitman," he said. "Get everything ready in the studio. I'll go."

Punctually at two in the afternoon, on this eventful day, the vast and gloomy station lay, like the temple of a dead religion, silent and deserted. Here and there a wandering footfall echoed. The main departure platform slumbered like the rest.

"I don't know if it strikes you as it does me, but the place seems deserted," said Pitman, peering anxiously around the empty station.

"Kind of a Jack-in-the-box feeling?" asked Michael, looking back at the main entrance with longing. "Five minutes ago I was still a lighthearted man walking the sunny streets of London, but now I feel as if all these empty trains might be filled with policemen waiting for a signal. It's guilt, Pitman."

In this uneasy frame of mind, they walked nearly the whole length of the departure platform, and at the far end became aware of a slender figure standing backed against a pillar. The figure was plainly deep in thought. He was not aware of their approach and continued gazing blankly across the empty tracks. Michael stopped.

"Wait a minute!" he said. "Can that be your advertiser? If so, I'm finished." And then, more cheerfully, "Not so either. Give me the spectacles."

"But you agreed I was to have them," protested Pitman.

"Ah, but that man knows me," said Michael.

"Does he? What's his name?" cried Pitman.

"You'll know soon enough," replied Michael. "But I may say one thing. If he's your advertiser, you can go ahead with a clear conscience, for I hold him in the palm of my hand."

The pair drew nearer to Morris.

"Are you looking for William Dent Pitman?" asked the artist. "I am he."

Morris raised his head. He saw standing before him, in the speaker, a person of almost indescribable insignificance. A little behind, stood a burly whiskered figure in spectacles. Ever since he had decided to call up devils from the underworld of London, Morris had pondered deeply on the probabilities of their appearance. His first emotion was one of disappointment. His second reaction was one of mild astonishment. Never before had he seen a couple so dressed. He had struck a new stratum.

"I must speak with you alone," he said.

"You need not mind my companion," replied Pitman. "He knows everything."

"Everything? Do you know what I am here to discuss?" asked Morris. "The barrel."

Pitman turned pale. "So you are the man!" he cried. "You very wicked person!"

"Can I speak openly in front of him?" asked Morris, disregarding Pitman's rebuke.

"He has been present throughout the affair," said

Pitman. "He opened the barrel. Your guilty secret is already known to him."

"Well, then," said Morris, "what have you done with the money?"

"I know nothing about any money," said Pitman.

"You needn't try that one," said Morris. "I have tracked you down. You came to the station in disguise, procured the barrel, opened it, rifled the body, and cashed the check. I have been to the bank, I tell you! I have followed you step by step, and your denials are childish and absurd."

"Come, come, Morris, keep your temper."

"Michael!" cried Morris. "Michael's here too?"

"Here too," echoed his cousin. "Here and everywhere. Every step you take is counted. Trained detectives follow you like your shadow. They report to me every hour. No expense is spared."

Morris' face took on a hue of dirty gray. "Well, I don't care. That man cashed my check!" he cried, pointing at Pitman. "It's a theft, and I want the money back."

"It was I alone who touched the body," began Michael.

"You? Michael!" cried Morris, stepping back. "Then why haven't you declared the death?"

"What the devil do you mean?" asked Michael.

"Am I mad, or are you?" cried Morris.

The three men stared at each other, wild-eyed.

"This is dreadful," cried Morris. "I can't seem to understand anything that is going on."

"I give you my word of honor, nor do I," said Michael.

"And why whiskers?" cried Morris, pointing in a ghastly manner at his cousin.

"Oh, that's a matter of detail," replied Michael. "Let's review the situation. My friend Pitman, here, received a barrel which, it now appears, was meant for you. The barrel contained the body of a man. How or why you killed him . . ."

"I never laid a hand on him," protested Morris. "This is what I dreaded all along. Yet you know I'm not that kind of man. With all my faults, I wouldn't touch a hair of anybody's head. He got killed in that vile train crash."

Suddenly Michael was seized by a laughter so excessive that his companions supposed beyond a doubt his reason had deserted him. Again and again, he struggled to compose himself, and again and again laughter overwhelmed him like a tide. Pitman and Morris, drawn together by common fear, exchanged glances of anxiety.

"Morris," gasped his cousin, when he was at last able to speak. "I see it all now. *I never guessed it was Uncle Joseph until this moment.*"

This remark produced an instant lightening of tension in Morris. For Pitman, it quenched the last ray of hope and daylight. Uncle Joseph, whom he had left an hour ago, pasting newspaper clippings? Uncle Joseph was the dead body? Then who was he, Pitman? Was this Waterloo Station or the madhouse?

"To be sure, the body was badly smashed!" cried Morris. "How stupid not to think of that. Why then, my dear Michael, we're both saved. You get the tontine. Your father is the last surviving beneficiary. I get the leather business. Declare the death at once, and we're all right."

"Ah, but I can't declare it," said Michael.

"Why not?" cried Morris.

"I can't produce the corpse, Morris. I've lost it," said his cousin.

"That's not possible!" exclaimed Morris, in dismay.

"Well, it's true," said Michael serenely. "Not recognizing the body, you see, and suspecting something irregular, I got rid of it at once."

"You got rid of the body? What made you do that?" wailed Morris. "But can you get it again? Do you know where it is?"

"I wish I did, Morris, but the fact is, I don't," replied Michael.

"Not again! I've lost the leather business again," moaned Morris.

Once more, Michael was overcome with laughter.

"Why do you laugh?" cried his cousin. "You lose more than I. The tontine has slipped from your hands. But I'll tell you one thing—that eight hundred pounds is mine and I want it now. Give it to me or I go straight to Scotland Yard and expose this whole disreputable story."

"Morris," said Michael, "it wasn't us, it was the other man. We never even searched the body."

"The other man?" repeated Morris.

"Yes, the other man. We palmed Uncle Joseph off on another man," said Michael. "He thought he was getting a piano."

Morris wiped his brow. It was wet with sweat. "Fever," he decided. "Who is this other man? How can I get hold of him?"

"Well, he's been in possession of the piano with the body since Wednesday, about four o'clock, and is now, I should imagine, on his way to New Zealand."

"Michael," said Morris pleadingly, "I am in a very weak state. Say it again slowly. When did he get it?"

Michael repeated his statement.

"Even the dates are sheer nonsense," said Morris thickly. "The check was cashed on Tuesday. The whole thing's without a gleam of reason."

A young gentleman, who had passed the trio and

suddenly started and turned back, at this moment laid a heavy hand on Michael's shoulder.

"Ah, so I've caught you at last," he said.

Michael, with his brand-new whiskers, broke from the grasp of the stranger and turned to run. Pitman followed his example with a bird-like screech. The stranger, finding the rest of his prey escape him, pounced roughly on Morris himself.

"I have one of the gang," said Gideon Forsyth.

"I don't understand," said Morris dully.

"Oh, I will make you understand," replied Gideon grimly.

"You will be a good friend to me if you can make me understand anything," cried Morris with conviction.

"I don't know you personally, do I?" continued Gideon, examining his unresisting prisoner. "Never mind, I know your friends. They are your friends, aren't they?"

"I don't understand," said Morris.

"You had something to do with a piano?" suggested Gideon.

"A piano!" cried Morris, clasping Gideon convulsively by the arm. "Then you're the other man! Where is it? Where is the body?"

"Where is the body? This is very strange," mused Gideon. "Do you want the body?"

"Want it!" cried Morris. "My whole fortune depends upon it! I lost it. Where is it? Take me to it!"

"Oh, you want it, do you? And the other man, does he want it, too?" asked Gideon.

"You mean Michael Finsbury? Why, of course he does! If he had it, he'd have won the tontine."

"Michael Finsbury! Not the lawyer?" cried Gideon.

"Yes, the lawyer," said Morris. "But where is the body?"

"I have lost it myself," replied Gideon.

CHAPTER XV

The Accomplice
Returns

MORRIS RETURNED FROM WATERLOO STATION in a frame of mind that baffles description. He was an ordinary man, but he had considered himself, until lately, to be fully equal to the demands of life. Today, he admitted defeat. Life had the upper hand. If there had been any means of flight or place to flee to, Morris would have instantly resigned all further claims on the rewards and pleasures of the world and, with inexpressible contentment, ceased to be. Just as the sick dog crawls under the sofa in search of solitude, so Morris could shut the door of John Street behind him.

Dusk was falling when he drew near this place of refuge. The first thing that met his eyes was the figure of a man. The man had no hat, and his clothes were hideous with filth. Yet Morris knew him at once. John had returned.

The first impulse of flight was replaced, in the elder brother's bosom, by the empty feeling of despair. "What does it matter now?" he thought.

John turned around. His face was ghastly with weariness and dirt and fury. As he recognized his brother, he drew in a long rasping breath and his eyes glittered.

"Open that door," he ordered, standing back.

"I am going to," said Morris warily.

The two brothers passed into the hall, closing the door behind them. Suddenly John seized Morris by the arm. "You mangy little cad!" he cried. "It would serve you right if I smashed your skull," he added, shaking Morris so violently that his teeth rattled in his head.

"It can't do you any good now, Johnny."

"Shut your mouth!" cried John. "Your time has come to listen."

He strode into the dining room, fell into the softest chair, and taking off one of his mud-encrusted shoes, nursed for a while his blistered foot like one in agony. "I'm lame for life," he said. "What is there for dinner?"

"Nothing, Johnny," said Morris.

" 'Nothing'? What do you mean by that?"

"I mean simply nothing," said his brother. "I have nothing to eat, and no money to buy anything. I've only had a cup of tea and a sandwich today myself."

"Only a sandwich?" sneered John. "I suppose *you're* the one to complain? But you had better take care. I've had all I mean to take. I tell you, I'm going to dine!"

"But if it's not possible, Johnny?" pleaded Morris.

"You nincompoop!" cried John. "Aren't we householders? Don't they know us at the corner hotel? Off with you! If you aren't back in a half hour, and if the dinner isn't good, first I'll beat you till you can't breathe, and then I'll go straight to the police and spill the story. Do you understand that, Morris Finsbury? Because if you do, you had better jump."

The idea of food appealed to even a wretched Morris, who was sick with famine. He sped upon his errand, and returned to find John still nursing his foot.

"What would you like to drink, Johnny?" he asked soothingly.

"A glass of port," John ordered imperiously. "And look here, light the fire and draw down the blinds. It's cold and it's getting dark. When you finish, start setting the table."

The room looked comparatively habitable by the time dinner came. It was a meal uncompromisingly British, but nourishing.

"Now," said John, his nostrils sniffing wide, "I'm going to sit here, and you are going to stand there, Morris Finsbury, and play butler."

"But, Johnny, I'm so hungry myself," pleaded Morris.

"You can have what I leave," replied his brother. There was something indescribably menacing in John's face as he uttered these words, at which the soul of Morris withered. "Do you know how I got here?" he asked, with another explosion of wrath.

"No, Johnny, how could I?" said Morris obsequiously.

"I walked on my ten toes!" cried John. "I tramped and begged all the way from Browndean. I would like to see you beg. It's not so easy as you might suppose. Pass the beef."

"Why didn't you stay at Browndean?" Morris ventured.

"I had to leave Browndean. I had to, I tell you," said John. "Nobody in his right mind could stay in a place like that. And then our landlord came nos-

ing around, wanting to know where the barrel
was. I told him to go to the devil. Then he said I
had pawned it, and did I know that was a felony?
And off he started to get the constable. There I
feel better now," he sighed, drawing his chair nearer to the fire. "So, with the constable coming and
all, I decided I was superfluous and shut the door
to that wretched cottage behind me forever. Pass
the cheese and that bottle of port. Michael was
right about this port. Now, there's a man for you.
He's clever and reads books. Speaking of Michael,
you've made a mess of it, eh?"

"Michael made a mess of it," Morris corrected.
"He has lost the body, and the death can't be
declared."

"Hold on," said John. "I thought you didn't want
to."

"Oh, we're far past that," said his brother. "It's
not the tontine now, it's the leather business, Johnny. It's the very clothes upon our backs."

"Tell your story from beginning to end," said
John, scratching his head solemnly.

Morris did as he was bid.

"Well, now, what did I tell you?" cried John.
"But I know one thing, I'm not going to be cheated
out of my property."

"I should like to know what you mean to do!"
exclaimed Morris.

"I'm going to put my interests in the hands of the smartest lawyer in London," said John, with decision. "Whether you go to jail or not is a matter of indifference to me."

"Why, Johnny, we're in the same boat!"

"Are we?" cried his brother. "You bet we're not! Have I committed forgery? Have I lied about Uncle Joseph? Have I put idiotic advertisements in the paper? Have I smashed other people's statues? I like your nerve, Morris Finsbury. No, I've let you run my affairs too long. Now they shall go to Michael."

At this moment, the brothers were interrupted by an insistent ringing at the door. With resignation, Morris accepted from the hands of a messenger a letter addressed in Michael's hand. Its contents ran as follows:

Morris Finsbury, be at my office at 10 a.m. tomorrow. *It is to your advantage.*
Michael Finsbury

So utter was Morris' surrender that he did not wait to be asked, but handed the note to John as soon as he had glanced at it himself.

"That's the way to write a letter," cried John. "Nobody but Michael could have written that."

And Morris did not even claim the credit of priority.

CHAPTER XVI

The Final Hour

THE FINSBURY BROTHERS were ushered into Michael's office promptly at ten the next morning. John was somewhat restored, but Morris was a man ten years older than the one who had left Browndean eight days before. His face was ploughed with anxious wrinkles, his dark hair was liberally streaked with gray.

Three persons were seated at a table to receive

them. Michael presided, with Gideon Forsyth to his right, and an old gentleman to his left.

"Why, it's Uncle Joseph!" cried John.

But Morris approached his uncle with glittering eyes and clenched fists.

"No use making trouble now," remarked Michael. "Look the facts in the face. Your uncle, as you see, was not as shaken in the accident as you might have imagined. A man of your humane disposition ought to be delighted."

"But what about the body?" wailed Morris, looking blankly about the room. "You don't mean to insinuate that thing I schemed and sweated for was the body of a total stranger?" he asked incredulously, sinking into a chair. "And to think that I would have found it out if the barrel had come to the house. Why didn't it? Why did it go to Pitman? What right had Pitman to open it?"

"And what right had you to open the packing case, Morris?" retorted Michael. "What have you done with the statue of Hercules?"

"He went through it with a sledge hammer," offered John.

"Well," snapped Morris, shoving his brother aside, "Uncle Joseph's alive, and I claim the tontine. Yes, I claim it now. I believe Uncle Masterson is dead."

"I must put a stop to this nonsense forever," said Michael. "My father is alive. Uncle Joseph saw him this morning."

"Yes, he still lives," said Joseph, with regret.

"So, you've lost again, Morris," said John. "What a fool you've made of yourself!"

"And that was why you wouldn't compromise!" cried Morris, turning to Michael.

"As for the absurd relationship in which you and Uncle Joseph find yourselves," continued Michael, "it is more than time it came to an end. I have prepared discharge papers which you shall sign."

"What!" cried Morris. "Lose my £7,800, the leather business, and the tontine? Thank you."

"It's like you to feel gratitude," began Michael.

"Oh, I know it's no good appealing to you, you sneering devil!" cried Morris. "But there's a stranger present, I can't think why, and I appeal to him. I was robbed of this money when I was an orphan. Since then, my only wish has been to reclaim what is rightfully mine."

"Morris," interrupted Michael, "I do wish you would let me add one point."

"Well, what is it?" asked Morris.

"It's only the name of one of the persons who's to witness your signature," replied Michael. "His name's Elgin."

There was a long silence. "I might have known it was you!" cried Morris.

"You'll sign, won't you?"

"Do you know what you're doing?" cried Morris. "You're compounding a felony."

"Very well, then, we won't compound it, Morris," said Michael. "See how little I understood the sterling integrity of your character! I thought you would prefer it so."

"Look here, Michael," interrupted John, "this is all very well and good, but how about me? I was a defrauded orphan too."

"Johnny," said Michael, "don't you think you should let me handle this?"

"I'm your man," said John. "I know you wouldn't deceive a poor orphan. Morris, you had better sign that document if you know what's good for you."

Morris nodded his head slowly in defeat. Clerks were brought in, the discharge was executed, and Joseph was a free man once more.

"And now, hear what I propose to do," said Michael. "Morris and John, the leather business has been assigned to the pair of you. And here is a check for the balance of your fortune. Now you see, Morris, you are no longer defrauded. You can start afresh. And here's kind regards from a Mr. Elgin."

Morris pounced on his check.

"I don't believe it," remarked John. "It seems too good to be true."

"It's simply a readjustment," Michael explained. "I've absorbed Uncle Joseph's liabilities. If he gets the tontine, it's to be mine. If my father gets it, it's mine in any case, you see. So, any way you look at it, I win the tontine."

"I always said you were clever," offered John.

"And now, Gideon," continued Michael, turning to his silent guest, "here are all the criminals before you, except Pitman. We're not pretty to look at. What do you propose to do with us?"

"Nothing in the world," replied Gideon. "I seem to gather that this wretched cousin of yours has already paid through the nose. And really, to be quite frank, I do not see who is to gain by any scandal."

"There's one thing more," added Michael. "I don't want you to misjudge poor Pitman, who is the most harmless being on earth."

"But can we do nothing for the man in the cart?" asked Gideon. "I have qualms of conscience."

"Nothing but sympathize," said Michael.